OF PATRIOTS AND TYRANTS

The Divided America Zombie Apocalypse
Book Two

B. D. Lutz

© 2020 B.D. Lutz.
ISBN: 978-1-7352793-0-5

This is a work of fiction. Names, characters, businesses, places, events, locales, and incidents are either the products of the author's imagination or used in a fictitious manner. Any resemblance to actual persons, living or dead, or actual events is purely coincidental. All rights reserved. No part of this publication may be reproduced, distributed, or transmitted in any form or by any means, including photocopying, recording, or other electronic or mechanical methods, without the prior written permission of the publisher, except in the case of brief quotations embodied in critical reviews and certain other non-commercial uses permitted by copyright law.

All rights reserved. Except as permitted under the U.S. Copyright Act of 1976, no part of this book may be reproduced, scanned, transmitted or distributed in any form or by any means, or stored in a database or retrieval system, without the prior written permission of the publisher. Please do not participate in or encourage piracy of copyrighted materials in violation of the author's rights.

Contact the author via email: CLELUTZ11@gmail.com

ACKNOWLEDGEMENTS

Edited by Monique Happy Editorial Services
www.moniquehappyeditorial.com

Thank you for your hard work and guidance. I know I don't make it easy on you and I can't believe you're not sick of me!

Cover designed by: Kelly A. Martin
www.kam.design
Kelly, you're a master at your craft!

Prologue

Packet entered the private quarters of Dear Leader. Much to his dismay, the man was showing the first signs of the virus ravaging his body. His pasty skin glistened with a sweet-smelling sweat while dark rings circled his eyes.

They should have tested the delivery method on a dope-fiend!

"Dear Leader, has your medical team failed to bring you the comfort you deserve?"

Dear Leader sat back hard in his throne-like chair. He cut a hard look at Packet and said, "The imbecile tested my remedy, as she always does. All seemed fine. I'm still strong, and not pleased with you, VC Packet."

Packet went off balance at the news of the young nurse. His vision swam while becoming fuzzy on its edges. He had just set the virus loose on his beloved DPRK. His mind raced. *No, no, no!* Only he and Dear Leader were to die today. Dear Leader gave a subdued but deep phlegm-rattling cough as Packet recovered from the shocking news.

"Packet, you dared to question me and my wisdom of leadership. You dared to ask me to wait for the imperial scum to *give approval* to the great DPRK." The repugnant toad turned his head sharply and let a violent cough go airborne. Dear Leader had never covered his vile little mouth when he expelled his DNA into the air. He once told Packet that it was considered an honor to have his fluids spread upon one's body. It brought that person strong wisdom.

This time, it brought a globule of dark green and black mucus that held no wisdom, only death.

"Packet, I've grown hungry. Do you have any food in the pockets of your shameful suit?"

Packet grew uncomfortable in the presence of the crazy little man. A substance bearing a strong resemblance to smegma was seeping through his pores, its warm-damp smell so pungent, Packet gagged. He realized Dear Leader was dying.

Packet decided today was not his day to die—it was in fact his day to lead! He seized the opportunity and said, "Dear Leader, it appears First Vice Chairman Choke had plans to remove you from office. I found his sample of the weapon still at his station. I also witnessed him speaking to the young nurse and her guard before they entered your greatness' quarters."

Dear Leader attempted to stand as anger filled his eyes, but only managed to raise an inch from his chair.

Packet continued, "You appear very sick, Dear Leader. With how quickly this set upon you, it must be the work of a traitor."

Dear Leader again attempted to stand and again he failed. As he reclaimed his seat, the sound of air escaping his body followed by the overpowering reek of feces filled the room.

Forty years of oppressed wrath bubbled over and pushed Packet forward with his quickly materializing plan. "Dear Leader, I possess the solution to your condition. Would you like to live, you fat little shit?"

Dear Leader's eyes burned with hatred at the insult. He opened his mouth to hurl odium at Packet, but his now purple tongue was swollen to three times its normal size, forcing his words to remain in his contaminated mouth.

"I'll take that as confirmation that you want to live. I'll be back in a moment. Keep still, my Dear Pig."

Packet left the room and walked directly to the typewriter in the adjoining room. He inserted Dear Leader's official letterhead and typed Dear Leader's proclamation:

> *Let it be known that I will be conducting Field Guidance then retreating to Mount Paektu to confer with Kim Il-sang. I place Vice Chairman Packet in power during this most important time in our history. I will return with enhanced knowledge and will crush all who oppose me under my fearsome fists.*
>
> *Dear Leader,*
> *Kim Jun-on*

Packet returned to the stench-filled room, memo in hand. "Sign this, and you live."

Dear Leader struggled to move from the chair, only to succumb to his own girth. Packet placed a pen in Dear Leader's hand, positioned the memo on a silver tray, and stepped back, phone in hand. He waved the vial of white powder for Dear Leader to see and screamed, "SIGN IT."

Lowering his weighty head, he managed, through great effort, to sign the memo. Packet took a picture of the momentous occasion.

Packet approached and said, "Open your filthy mouth to receive the solution."

Dear Leader forced his mouth open and Packet poured the vial of weaponized heroin on his purple, distended tongue.

He snatched the struggling man's cell phone from the table, positioned next to his chair, and thanked him for his generosity. Packet exited the room to the delightful sounds of Dear Leader dying.

As the door slammed shut behind him, he dialed First Vice Chair Choke from Dear Leader's phone. The power he now possessed was infinite.

We will crush the imperial west, and I will lead us to victory. His revelry cut short when Choke's voice crackled through the phone's speaker.

Chapter 1
Not Much Has Changed

It's been two hours since we holed up in the basement of this abandoned house. We've gone *nose-blind* to the nasty food smell while the jokes about it have finally subsided. We've been working on a plan to get out of said basement, back to our Humvee then to Hazelton and ultimately home.

The whole situation has been wrong from the time we arrived in Hazelton, West Virginia until we picked up the two, now dead or possibly undead, refugees in Terra Alta, West Virginia. We can't correct the interference our radio is encountering. Our other radios, basically really good walkie-talkies, don't have the range to reach Camp Hazelton. I'm convinced that even if they did, we wouldn't get help anytime soon. After seeing what was happening at Right Entry Point One, the absolute crush of the living and UC trying to push through that gate, I doubt we ranked on any kind of priority list at Camp Hazelton.

The UC herds that cut us off from our exit are now pressed up against the house whose basement we're hiding in. All possible UC entry points are guarded; the challenge is that they're also our exit points. Most are small windows at ground level. It would take some hellacious maneuvering to squeeze our bodies through them. The ones giving us the most heartburn also hold the most potential for our escape. They comprise the basement entrance from the main floor and the cellar door on the north side of the basement. The main entrance to the single-story house faces south. From what we can tell, the cellar door has the largest amount of UCs congregating around it.

The UC crowd wasn't dispersing, but they weren't as agitated as they had been when they chased us into the house. That noise they recently started making made it hard to focus. My brain started walking along the road of *what ifs*. A dark bumpy road I find myself on far too often. I'm convinced I do it on purpose to see if I can drive myself insane! So, *what if* they're communicating? That would be a humdinger of a development. If they can communicate, how long until they start strategizing? The thought was scary enough to set my stomach to rumbling.

We fortified the two weak points using old shelving units and the boxes upon boxes of the nasty-smelling sausage-like substance. With no plans to eat it, we may as well put it to use saving our lives. Will, Jax, and Lisa were working on securing the doors while Stone, Randy, and I worked up an exit plan.

Our planning repeatedly produced the same result. Create a diversion to draw the UC crowd to one side of the house while we exit through the other side. It sounded simple enough. It would only take flawless execution on our part coupled with a willingness to cooperate on the UCs' part. *No worries, we got this.*

We decided that exiting through the main house was a better idea than going through the cellar doors in the basement. The doors are classic, old-school, sloped-wall cellar doors that offer no visibility to the outside and are positioned only a few inches off the ground. We'd be forced to bust through them at a full run to even give ourselves the slightest chance of making it to the Humvee. We have zero INTEL on the numbers of UC we're facing. No good sightline to the outside and exiting through the house would provide cover while the herd is distracted.

Now, we need to determine how to distract them. We carry a lot of things that go BANG, but employing them effectively is the challenge. Simply shooting through the windows won't work. The sound will just bounce around the basement, not drawing the UC to any specific area.

I looked at Stone and said, "We need a solid plan. Are you working on anything in that super-brain of yours?"

Stone shot me a puzzled look after my question, then Jax walked over to us, looking green and sweaty, he said "I think I have a plan."

Chapter 2
Dillan and Those Yankees Fans!

Dillan picked up the radio and asked Al to slow down and repeat his transmission. Al did as Dillan directed, but he only calmed down a little after he said, "We have UCs at the gate and dozens along the fence. They're stretching east about ten yards, two deep in some spots."

Dillan's gut clenched. He was convinced the gate would hold. In the earliest days of this nightmare, it had held steady for them. But the activity was picking up and the instances of UC sightings and contacts had also increased. He closed his eyes and wished he could just enjoy this rare half day off. He'd just sat down to catch up on his reading and pretend life was back to normal.

Dillan radioed back. "Crazy question. Can you describe what they're wearing?"

It was a solid thirty seconds before Al answered. "Shit, several have on New York shirts, like tourists, but I see several in New York Yankees gear. It's that same group we spotted a couple weeks ago, right?"

Dillan dragged his left hand down his face as he contemplated the situation and the directions he would give. He asked, "Did any of the towers see them approach? I didn't hear any shots fired. So I'm guessing no."

Al paused and said, "They approached from the direction of the Center Tower, during shift change. We heard what sounded like a large engine, possibly a truck, and assumed Otto and his crew had already returned." Al paused to catch his breath and slow himself down before continuing. "We tried to locate the source of the noise and that slowed down the shift change. By the time we realized the truck was a street to our north, the UCs were pouring through the trees headed right at us. The trees also blocked our view of the truck."

Dillan held his emotions in check. His crew had been doing an excellent job with little training and even less sleep, so he would not call them out on this. Plus, it sounded like they had been observed and sabotaged by someone, but why? He didn't have the answer, but he knew things needed to change at the gate and fence. He'd bring back the hidden watchers and start staggering the shift changes. Someone had figured out the timing and exploited it.

Dillan broke the thought when his radio squawked. "Dillan, this is Northeast Tower. I caught a glimpse of the truck; it was military size but solid black. It didn't look like a RAM military truck. It went north after it dropped the UCs."

With that news, Dillan started barking orders: "Northeast and Northwest Towers, thin the back of the crowd; keep your fire a safe distance from the fence. Southeast, Southwest and South-Center, keep your heads down and use your binoculars for all viewing. We can't let this be used as a distraction to launch an attack. Shoot anyone, except Otto's group and our military friends, on sight."

He took a deep breath, put his book down and started for the door. He grabbed his gun belt and rifle as he brought his radio to his mouth and called out to the foot patrols. "Patrol One, split into two pair. Help cover the south and east fences." The foot patrols comprised four groups of four well-armed men and women. They walked the perimeter and interior of the community looking for threats and were morphing into a small police force.

He received confirmation from Patrol One and keyed the radio again. "Patrol Two, split into pairs as well; cover the west and north fences. All of you keep your heads on swivels and shoot anything that looks out of place." Dillan headed to the north fence, gradually increasing his pace as his anxiety built.

His commands coming much faster now, he again raised the two-way and said, "Patrol Three, get the supply Jeep going and circle the community in a random pattern. Be ready to respond to any calls for backup from the patrols or the towers."

The confirmations of understanding came fast and furious from all the patrols. Dillan nodded in approval and broke into a full run.

Suddenly, a Black Hawk and two Boeing AH-6 Little Birds, outfitted with rocket and Gatling-gun pods, passed overhead, northbound at what appeared to be full speed. Praying that the appearance of the helicopters was only a coincidence, he continued towards the action. As he rounded the corner that would bring him to the gate, he heard the commotion before he saw it— and then his blood began to boil.

Chapter 3
Caught In The Act

Captain Riggins heard it first; then John did a moment later. Faintly at first, but quickly growing in volume—the sound was unmistakable. They would see them any second. Helicopters, most likely RAM military copters. This wouldn't end well for the defenseless tugs. The fleet only carried small arms, which were no match for the hellfire speeding their way.

They'd set sail in a group of five, all of them overflowing with the deadly cargo they'd been hauling for weeks now. The captain had had a bad feeling when they left port today, so bad he allowed the other tugs to take the lead. It appeared his feeling had been more of a premonition. They were going to die today.

An idea crashed into his head, and it might just buy John and him a little time.

"John, get the large tarp out of storage and get it to the deck. Grab any paint or grease we have in storage… do it NOW." The captain was screaming by the time he finished, and John flinched at the volume and urgency. He started moving immediately. Captain Riggins grabbed the keys to the locker where he kept his hunting rifle. It would prove futile against the copters, but if he was going to die, he'd die fighting.

John arrived on deck and dropped the supplies just short of Captain Riggins. The copters came into view and his eyes widened as he watched one of the small copters break formation and descend, at a slight angle, towards the furthest tug. He could see small arms fire ascending toward the speedy and nimble machine, but the rounds passed the copter well off target.

As the copter pivoted to face the tug and pulled into a hover, rockets burst from its sides. The tug lifted out of the water as flames shot into the sky, the shock wave pushing the remainder of the tugs around like toys in a swimming pool. A burst of heat washed over John, even though they were the last tug in the procession, hundreds of yards away from the carnage. He winced and raised his arms over his face, fearing his skin would blister.

The captain spun to face John, his face a wild mixture of fear and rage. He screamed at John, "Snap out of it and spread the tarp out on the deck. We can live through this, but you need to listen to me and—"

John interrupted him. "Why aren't we trying to escape?"

"They'll be on us in seconds," the captain shot back. "No time, John. Move if you want to live."

A second then third tug were sent to the bottom in fiery heaps. The broken bodies of their crews scattered over the water as their deadly cargo followed them to the murky depths of Lake Erie. The tug closest to them started a full reverse, heading directly for them.

Captain Riggins frantically used a mixture of paint and grease to write one word on the tarp. He screamed at John to cut the cargo free and turn hard to port. John released the rigging and cut so hard to port it felt like the tug might capsize. When he raised his head from the helm, he looked directly into the panicked eyes of the approaching tug's captain. John hadn't acted quickly enough, and he braced for impact.

Chapter 4
Jackson Hammer

Jack rubbed the sleep away as the heavenly aroma of coffee drifted in the air, bringing a sense of normalcy with it. Jack chuckled. "*Normal.* What's that even mean these days?"

He supposed normal was relative in today's world. The world in which he'd killed his neighbor and his only focus was on survival. *Normal* meant something different every day in this new life.

He paused to gaze at the pictures on the walls of the hall leading to the living room. The smiling faces of his family stared back at him. Pictures of good days in better times. He missed his brothers, Stone and Otto. The picture of the three of them on the couch in their childhood home sporting '80s mullets and porn-star mustaches was his favorite.

For years he'd assumed his brothers were paranoid. Now, as Otto pointed out, they were the smartest guys in the room. He'd never hear the end of it. Then he looked at the picture of Otto with a giant circular welt on his forehead. Otto got it from trying to smash a full can of beer using that thick skull of his. Jack was not afraid to use the picture to prove Otto might not be so smart after all. A crooked smile creasing his face at the thought, he made a mental note to try to make contact with them today. It had been over ten days since the last contact, and he worried about their safety. *Please let the cells work today.*

The coffee machine made the telltale gurgling indicating that the delicious dark liquid was ready for consumption. He intended to do just that after his morning security check. The picture window overlooking his property was still ten feet away when it became clear something was wrong. His gut clenched as his stride quickened.

"No, no, no, please no," he whispered as the view of his yard registered in his brain. "Where did you come from?" he asked the empty room. "How did so many of you get into my goddamn yard?" *Coffee, that's it, I need to wake up and I need coffee. This isn't real,* he thought. He arrived at the coffeemaker the same instant as his wife, Natalia.

"Who were you talking to? Did you finally get in touch with your brothers?" she asked.

"Natalia, get the ready bags and empty backpacks. Fill the backpacks with as much food as possible. Meet me in the garage in fifteen minutes."

Natalia's stunned look gave way to grim determination as she ran upstairs to begin packing without question. She knew what this meant. They'd talked about it at length.

Jack poured coffee into a huge travel mug and took a giant, blisteringly hot gulp. He ran back to the window only to find the coffee didn't help. The view hadn't changed; they had been overrun. His front yard held roughly a hundred UCs. They shambled aimlessly through his meager garden, bouncing off one another as they inched closer to his home. He found it odd that he didn't recognize a single one of them. In this small rural town, he knew all of his neighbors.

"Natalia, we need to move!" he yelled.

Chapter 5
Andy Has The Answer

Andy watched through the bedroom window of his quarantine house as Otto and the others left the gate. He was angry that he couldn't join them and despondent that he remained separated from his family, confused by how he felt both physically and mentally. The boredom was crushing him, his illness was scaring him; it became an endless cycle.

Sabrina and Durrell Adams make up the community's medical team. Both paramedics before the virus hit, they established what served as the community hospital. And they made house calls.

Sabrina and Durrell alternated their daily visits to Andy, attempting to limit their exposure to him. He received a concoction of antibiotics and antiviral medications in the hopes that whatever he was suffering from would respond. To date, they'd merely slowed the progression of his illness. They were baffled by his symptoms, which at times resembled the flu. They were at a loss to explain some of his other symptoms, including his slightly opaque skin-tone. But one symptom stood out among the others: his low body temperature. At ninety-seven degrees, he was at the lowest limit of the acceptable range with zero fluctuation. Any lower and hypothermia would set in.

"Are you cold, Andy?" Durrell asked. "You don't appear to have the chills, but you should with your internal temperature at ninety-seven degrees. Do you feel nauseous or unable to eat?"

Andy stood up from the couch while answering. "No, it's like every single day since being scratched. I feel off, that's the only way I'm able to describe it. Just feeling off."

Durrell began packing up the medical kit and asked, "How are your energy levels? I mean, you look fit, you aren't suffering atrophy of your limbs, and your weight hasn't fluctuated a single ounce. Do your energy levels match what I see?"

Andy was growing tired of the endless questions, the same questions every day. He wanted to rejoin his family, but he figured the community wouldn't allow it until they had some idea of what was going on.

"Durrell, I'm still working out every day. And I have an abundance of energy. I've increased my weight and reps when I lift. I'm on the treadmill for an hour, three times a day. Honestly, I think I could run a marathon tomorrow."

Durrell rubbed his temples, searching for answers, but found nothing. His frustration at not finding the root cause of Andy's illness had grown more pronounced over the last week. Not being an actual doctor was merely part of the issue. He was capable of diagnosing most common ailments or treating injuries ranging from bumps and scrapes to level one trauma. Virology and bacteriology, however, were disciplines far beyond his medical training. Add to his knowledge gap the absence of proper testing facilities and you had the current and extremely frustrating situation.

They'd spoken with Corporal Lewis about traveling to the local hospital to gain access to the facilities which Andy needed most. The response they'd received was bone-chilling. Lewis said that all hospitals were under heavy guard by a combination of militias and regular Army. They had orders to *sterilize* anyone with an unidentified illness. Meaning, the person doesn't even have the opportunity to enter the hospital proper. Medical staff would triage them in a remote location to determine their condition. If the person displayed any symptoms related to the virus, they would segregate them for further testing. If they were determined to be infected, or the illness was un-diagnosable, they were humanely terminated. *Humanely terminated.* The phrase punched Durrell square in the face.

Lewis subtly let them know that they were also under orders to terminate anyone showing symptoms that fell outside the norm. Unless, of course, the situation was being contained. Durrell and Sabrina guaranteed him that Andy would stay *contained* as long as the *humanely terminate* and or *sterilize* orders remained in place.

Durrell figured it was time to ask the question on everyone's mind. "Andy, do you feel like you want to eat humans? Just grab hold of one of us and put the grub on?"

Surprisingly unfazed, Andy replied, "Put the *grub* on? What the hell does that mean, Durrell? If the question is, do I want to eat your brains, the answer is no." Sensing Durrell's discomfort with the question, Andy said, "Now, if you're talking about putting the grub on a nice human neck, that's a different story." Durrell's eyes went wide at the statement; he opened his mouth to speak when Andy interrupted. "How much do you weigh, Durrell? You look to be about six-foot even and one-ninety, maybe two hundred pounds. Not counting your brain, of course."

Andy had slipped into a silky-smooth voice, almost like he was romancing a young lady at a bar. The questions and change in Andy's voice combined to send Durrell into an anxiety attack. He began sweating profusely and tried to respond. Instead, he sounded like a strobe-light might sound if strobe-lights could talk. "Andy, hey now, what's the, I mean, come on, and how would you, really now, really, come on."

Andy maintained eye contact and then finally he spoke. "Durrell, relax man. I'm just screwing with you. You look like you're going to bust a goiter… and that would just make me hungry."

As Andy burst out laughing, Durrell slammed his shin into a coffee table, yelping in pain, as he bolted for the door. Andy, now in tears with laughter, said, "Durrell, honestly, I'm just messing around. I don't have any crazy cravings for flesh." Then, taking a more serious tone, he said, "But I would like to see my wife. Can she and the kids move in here with me? I miss them, man."

Durrell let loose a string of obscenities that would have a truck driver blushing. He also determined that at this very second, Andy was his least favorite person on the planet. Yes, that included the hungry UCs running around the streets. "Andy, that was NOT COOL, not at all. You're a little jerk is what you are, scaring a man half-to-death. I damn near broke my leg because of that shit. God almighty, I may just hate you. Tell you what I'm going to do. I'm going to stop your food service. How would you like that? Jerk!" he said while limping to the door. Then, stopping before he exited, he said, "I'll talk to Pat and Darline, but I don't think it'll be a problem to have your family move in with you. I'm not sure why they'd want to see you, nasty little dude that you are. But a family should be together."

Andy said, "Durrell, the real answer is that I truly don't want to eat humans. I just feel off."

Durrell nodded and continued out the door. Andy stood alone in the living room and thought, *The problem is, Durrell, I feel better than I ever have in my life and I don't know why.*

Chapter 6
It's What You Know Not Who You Know

John closed his eyes and braced for impact. What happened was far less devastating than he'd expected. The oncoming tug had also corrected its course to avoid impact with the captain's tug, resulting in a glancing blow to the tug's starboard side which pushed it even further to port. The blow tossed John around the tug's bridge, slamming him against a wall, then to the deck. Starbursts of pain filled his eyes as he made contact with the unyielding hardwood.

After realizing that the worst had passed, John rose to his feet to survey the damage. The tug wasn't listing, which was a good sign that they weren't taking on water. With the number of zombies floating in the lake, the thought of abandoning ship terrified him.

As he watched the offending tug motor further away, a whooshing sound filled the air. He knew immediately what would follow. He slammed himself back to the deck and covered his head with his arms. Intense heat and a flash so bright it pierced the lids of his closed eyes followed the deafening explosion. He felt the tug move as the shockwave pushed it harder to port.

Once again he stood to look for damage. The other tug had been obliterated. Debris pelted his tug with pieces so large they smashed through the deck. He scrambled to the bow to find the captain and check the hull for damage. Panic set in as the reality hit him. The captain was nowhere in sight and the bow was pitching forward. The hull had been breached!

Rushing around the bow and yelling for the captain, he noticed one of the salvage lines stretched tight. He followed it to the side of the tug and looked over the edge to find the captain hanging by his right foot. It had become tangled in the line and now held him inches from the zombie-laden water.

With his back against the tug's hull, the captain pulled his head up to see John staring, wide-eyed, at him. "John, for Christsake, pull me up. We don't have time for this."

John had the captain back on the boat with one pull of the salvage line. The moment the captain got his footing on the deck, he was off like a shot, leaving the salvage line attached to his ankle. He grabbed one side of the tarp and yelled out, "John, get your ass in gear. Grab the tarp and hold it up facing the copters."

John ran to the tarp and did as ordered. They both stretched their bodies to gain the height needed to display the message on the tarp.

All three copters pulled to a hover directly in front of the tug, then a blinding spotlight focused on the tarp. John prepared to die in a fiery explosion, but nothing happened. A voice broke over a loudspeaker: "This is Chief Warrant Officer Albright. Prepare to be taken into custody."

John couldn't believe they were still alive. He looked over at the captain, who gave him a grim nod. They set the tarp down and John read the single word scribbled on its slick surface.

Information.

Chapter 7
Battle Cry

"Jax, you okay? You're looking a little peaked," I said after he told us he had a plan to get us out of this horrible basement. He was slick with sweat and struggled to remain upright. "What's up Jax? Talk to us, man."

Jax tried to generate some saliva but the action only produced a pasty-wet sound when his lips parted. "I need some water, Otto. I'm parched."

The five of us searched our packs for a bottle of water. He accepted Lisa's offering and downed nearly the entire bottle in three large gulps before saying, "Otto, I think I'm turning into a UC."

The revelation stunned the team, and true to form, I panicked and said, "Jax, you're not turning. It's the heat, you're just over-heating, right? We haven't had air-conditioning for weeks. You've got all that gear on; you probably ate a nasty MRE for breakfast. The heat and the food are combining to make you sick. You're fine." I tend to babble at the mouth in high-pressure situations.

Randy looked at me like I had lobsters crawling from my left ear. "Otto, are you sure you're feeling okay today? You keep doing that. It's like your brain and mouth disconnect from your head. Then your mouth assumes it's free to start blurting out words. It's creeping me out."

Jax cut in. "We need to get moving." He pulled the collar of his ACU from his neck to display a nasty-looking scratch. "I don't have much time. I can feel it burning through my body. One of them got hold of me. Only a tiny nick, but apparently that's all you need. I feel like shit."

"NOOO, damn it all to hell, no!" Stone bellowed at the sight of the wound. He and Jax had become fast friends during our training. Still, his reaction caught me off guard. Stone had always held his emotions in check. No matter the circumstances, he stayed focused and reserved. The prospect of losing Jax appeared to break down his defenses and open him to the raw emotion of the moment.

Jax either ignored the reaction from Stone and the team, or it simply didn't register. He began laying out the plan in a raspy-wet voice, similar to the sound the UCs made.

A million questions slammed around my head as he spoke. I needed to know if it hurt and what *feeling like shit* actually felt like? Did he want to eat me, or another team member before me? If so, why not me first? Did that mean he was saving the best for last? Did UCs get full if they ate too much? At what point did he realize something was wrong (probably the only useful question in my head).

I was pulled from my trance when Lisa hit me in the chest. "Let's go," she said, locking eyes with me. I became aware of a flurry of activity in the basement. Jax asked Randy for two flash-bangs; Stone was removing the blockade from the cellar doors. Will was loading magazines and the M249's ammo pouch and function-checking our weapons. Curiously, he also had bladed- and blunt-force weapons piled next to the magazines.

Lisa again said, "Let's go, Otto. We need to move NOW."

She's so loud. "Go where?" I asked.

Her eyes bugged out. I thought they might pop out and smack me in the face. "OTTO, are you kidding me?" she screamed, her body shaking with frustration. "Did you get poor marks in grade school for paying attention? Or maybe your mom dropped you on your head as a baby?" Snapping her fingers, she said, "That's it. Your tiny brain is damaged from being dropped on that fragile skull of yours."

"Well, that was mean," I said.

She hit me in the chest again and told me to just start moving, to do something useful. It became clear that I had, in fact, been in my own head so deeply that I had missed the plan. You know, the plan that could save our lives.

"What's my part?" I asked.

"You're on my six while I breach the exit to the main floor," she answered.

"What's the full plan?" I asked while finally finding the brain-power to jolt my legs to action.

"Otto, if we didn't need to get moving, I'd smack the taste out of your mouth for asking that question. We, me and you, breach the door and clear a path. Stone and Will cover the stairs while Jax exits the cellar door and draws the UCs to him."

The plan felt like someone had punched me in the gut. Jax was sacrificing his life for us. I looked at him while he readied himself. It was evident he was succumbing to the virus. He glanced at me, still managing a wink, then turned and walked to the doors.

"We have to do this now. When you hear the gunshot, you're out of time," Jax said, barely above a raspy whisper.

Looking around the room at each of us, he followed with, "Be the storm."

Stone moved toward him, but Jax waved him off. He turned and smashed his body into the door and pushed with his last shred of strength.

As the door began to open, Stone put his hand on Lisa's shoulder and said, "Change in plans. I'm on point, Otto's on my six." His delivery left no room for debate. He pivoted to me saying, "Just like Saturday night in the Flats." I understood what he meant; I was ready.

This fight would be up-close, personal, and brutal.

Club in hand, he ascended the stairs. Stealth was imperative for our plan to work. Gunfire would draw them to us, rendering Jax's sacrifice meaningless. I pulled my extendable baton from my MOLLE vest. With a flick of my wrist, it extended to its full twenty-one inches. Two steps at a time, I followed Stone to the entrance. We paused at the threshold; I didn't know why. I would have if I'd actually listened to the plan. Deciding to keep my mouth shut and avoid another incident like the one with Lisa, I waited in silence.

The explosion of activity proved as violent as the explosion that set it in motion. The first flash-bang's detonation cued Stone to burst through the door with me on his heels. Stone let loose a battle cry as gunfire erupted from the basement.

Chapter 8
All Is Lost

"Jackson Hammer, maybe we could pack faster if you stopped staring at your precious garden being destroyed, AND ACTUALLY HELPED. I'm moving as fast as I can while you drink coffee in your PJs. So, stop staring and start moving."

Jack realized what the tone… yah, the *tone*, Natalia used meant. He was in trouble. No, it didn't matter that they were being overrun and might die. She was mad and would stay mad until he corrected whatever wrong he had committed. But she had a point, he should probably change. Dying in PJs didn't seem a manly way to go.

He finally yanked his attention away from the window and his garden and headed for the kitchen. Not knowing when he would be able to drink coffee again, he stopped and topped off his mug. Natalia's voice hit a fevered pitch, and he bolted for the stairs.

Arriving in their bedroom, he found Natalia had them nearly ready to abandon their home. He headed to the drawer and grabbed the two handguns they owned and handed one to Natalia. "Is the ammo packed up?" he asked as he press-checked his Smith & Wesson M&P to ensure a round was chambered.

"I don't know Jackson, is the AMMO PACKED UP?"

He really was in trouble this time. "Got it, I'll grab it. Should I grab anything else before I ask another stupid question?"

Natalia threw an empty backpack at him and yelled, "FILL IT."

He retreated to the kitchen and began filling the bag with canned and dry goods. The backpack filled quickly, and he took it to the interior entrance to the attached garage and left it. Running back upstairs, he met Natalia as she descended.

"More. Upstairs. Go!" she told him as he approached her. He continued past her, not making eye contact so she didn't yell at him again. Once upstairs, he grabbed the remaining bag and two boxes of ammo. He realized that he should have bought more when his brothers told him it was on sale. He'd never hear the end of it. Of course he'd need to live long enough for his brothers to bust his chops. And living long enough started with him picking up the pace.

Natalia was waiting at the door, looking less than pleased that the simple task seemed to take him forever. He dropped the bag and told her to hold on.

"What are you doing, Jackson? They are literally at our windows; they know we're in here." As if on cue, the sound of breaking glass filled the house.

This wasn't supposed to happen. They lived so far away from population centers that they'd thought they were safe. How had this happened? They'd lost everything they'd worked for and might lose more if they didn't get out now.

As Jack opened the door leading to the garage, the lights flickered then went dark. "Are you kidding me?" he exclaimed. The power in their area hadn't been as reliable as it was by his brother's homes. For the last three days they had been running the generator nearly non-stop. Part of his morning routine, the one interrupted by this fiasco, was topping it off with fuel. A full tank usually lasted a full twenty-four hours. And it seemed that twenty-four hours had just expired. With the generator located outside, refilling it now was out of the question.

More glass breaking was followed this time by a loud thud.

"JACKSON, I love you, but I will leave you behind if you don't do something."

A little shocked, Jack answered, "Leave me behind? Really, just leave me here to die a horrible death because I didn't moooove fast enough for your liking?"

Natalia responded, "I'm not getting eaten, Jackson, so move or I'll use you as bait for my escape."

This was coming at them fast, too fast. But he thought Natalia was being a little harsh by threatening to leave him behind. Or to use him as bait. He'd get them out of this; he just needed a second to clear his head.

He pushed the rest of the way through the door and said, "After you, my loving wife." The comment got him a sharp look and more contact than was necessary as she pushed by him and into the garage. The first UC rounded the corner from the living room as he started to shut the door behind them. He looked back at the monster and noticed the keys to his truck hanging on the key-hook over the UCs left shoulder. *Natalia isn't going to be happy about this,* he thought as the UC hit the door, slamming it shut.

Chapter 9
All About The Follow-Through

Stone made contact with the first UC while his battle cry roared from his lungs. The blow was so brutal the UC's head exploded like an overripe melon. He pivoted left, landing another devastating blow on the next UC shambling in our direction. The upper floor held only a handful of UCs, all of which blocked our exit. The basement door opened to a short hallway between the kitchen and living room. Lisa shouted that Jax was drawing the herd toward the rear of the house where the kitchen was located. We needed to clear the living room for our escape double quick.

After the second UC fell to Stone's vicious attack, I turned to ensure no monsters had slipped in behind us. With no UCs showing their nasty mugs at our six, I joined Stone.

"Otto, kill the two on the right. I'll kill the bastards on the left."

As Stone finished the sentence, the UCs became aware of the fresh meat in the room and advanced on us as one. We moved out of the tight hallway, into the living room, and launched our attack on the unwelcome house guests. With a wet *thunk* I sent the first UC I faced to the floor. One problem: My baton went with it and so did I. On my way to the floor I realized that the energy from my blow to the side of its head had forced the baton deep into its skull, wedging it between broken and jagged bone.

When I hit the floor, I thought, *Son-of-a-bitch, how do I always end up on the ground!* Thankfully, the blow had ended the UC's life because I landed less than an inch from its mouth. Had it survived, I would have presented an easy meal. As I struggled to both free the baton and get to my feet, the second UC landed on my back, pushing me forward just enough to keep my neck out of bite-range.

I twisted to my left while pulling my fixed-blade Bowie knife from its sheath with my right hand. The action was smoother than I anticipated, and I quickly plunged the blade through the top of its head. I was feeling pretty good about myself, you know, smooth execution while under pressure and managing to not stab myself or get bit. I became aware that Stone's battle raged on and I figured I should offer my obviously superior fighting skills to him. I replaced the Bowie, yanked the baton loose and readied myself to re-enter the fight. The gunfire in the basement had stopped, and I figured it was now or never.

I jumped to my feet and found myself facing a window. The UCs surrounding the front of the house had thinned out considerably—an indication the plan was working. The second flash-bang detonated an instant later. Time to smash some UC heads; I turned in Stone's direction just in time to see the end of his club heading at my blocky head. I had, indeed, turned directly into Stone's follow-through swing. My last thought was, *That's going to leave a mark...* then everything went black.

Chapter 10
Airborne

"Captain Alexander Riggins," he said in response to Chief Warrant Officer Albright's question. "Where are you taking us? We have information and need to speak to the person running RAM."

Albright looked sharply at Riggins. "Captain, shut up," he said, then turned his attention to John. "What's your name?"

John hesitated, unsure if he should respond with the truth, or at all. He decided to follow the captain's lead. "John Lawson."

"Well, Riggins and Lawson, you were less than three seconds from joining the others from your group at the bottom of the lake." An explosion interrupted Albright. He cocked his head in a manner that told the men he was listening to something on his headset. "Riggins, your tug has been sanitized." The captain didn't flinch at the news; he had anticipated it and felt a strange sense of freedom when Albright confirmed the tug was gone.

Albright addressed them both. "Your actions have caused the senseless deaths of hundreds of RAM citizens. Your BSU government has achieved a new level of degeneracy, and you enabled them to do so. If it were up to me, I'd cut your throats and toss you into that mass of UCs from your tug. Lucky for you, it's not my call. Sit still and keep your mouths shut until we deliver you to our CO. You so much as twitch and I will end you both."

The copter dipped hard to port, giving Riggins and Lawson a clear view of the lake and the burning tugs below as the destruction came into full view. Flames licked the water's surface as thousands of undulating bodies reached for the copter in vain. The captain looked at John and nodded his head as the Black Hawk banked hard and accelerated away from the devastation.

Chapter 11
Old, Not Dead

I came to staring at the ground while being jostled roughly back and forth. Stone called someone a fat-ass, and it became clear a moment later he was talking about me. He was fireman-carrying me over grass. *He ain't heavy, he's my brother* popped into my head and I started to sing the song out loud. At which point Stone dropped me on my rear-end. "Get up and run, you lunatic. And don't sing another word of that song because you ARE heavy."

When I hit the ground my surroundings and the situation sank in. We had exited the house and were heading to the Hummer. The plan had worked. At a high cost, but it worked. Lisa was on point, Randy followed a few feet behind her, and Will was on our six. The formation, I assumed, was because I'd managed to get myself knocked out and they needed to cover Stone as he carried me to safety.

When I stood, we heard a single gunshot. As Jax had said, we were out of time.

Lisa yelled, "Move out." Stone handed me my AR and started running. I lingered a moment and looked back at the house, saying a silent prayer for Jax. Will gave me a push in my shoulder as he passed, letting me know I needed to fall in with the others.

We made it to the razor-wire barrier a minute later. The razor-wire was laid directly on the ground and strung between what appeared to be tank barriers, similar to what was used in World War II. The razor-wire stood roughly twenty inches high, with its blades glinting in the late afternoon sun. I was already intimidated.

Lisa pulled her ACU jacket off and covered the wire as best she could. Taking three steps back, she sprinted forward and leaped over the wire like a gazelle, hitting the other side where she tucked and rolled to a stop. On her feet in a flash, she took up a defensive position to cover us while we attempted the same maneuver. Will, Stone, and Randy cleared the barrier with little problem. It's amazing how motivated the threat of being eaten alive can make you.

I took the same path as the others, but as I launched myself into the air, I drifted left of Lisa's ACU. I knew immediately it would end badly for me. The others had leaped over with relative grace, executing perfect tuck and rolls when landing. I went over flailing like a man drowning in the middle of a lake. As I crested the peak of the barrier, my left bootlace caught on a blade, slamming me forward and onto my face. Son-of-a... did that hurt. I elevated my face from the ground (again) and tried to pull my boot free. The blade wouldn't relinquish its grip, holding me in a freakish warrior-three yoga pose. If I struggled much more, the blades were sure to start ripping into my ACUs and then the flesh they covered.

I hate stitches and decided to swallow my pride. "A little help would be nice," I said. The lack of response shocked me. The four of them just stood around apparently waiting for the razor-wire fairy to intervene. "Really, people? This is how you treat a member of your team?" I asked while looking up at them.

Stone finally took a knife and cut the laces of my boot, setting me free.

Lisa looked me up and down and said, "Well, I guess I only promised Darline I'd keep you alive. I made her no guarantees on the condition you'd be in when you got home."

I was a mess. The tongue of my boot flopped around, I was covered in mud, my nose was bleeding, and I had a giant bump on my head where Stone's club had made contact.

"You look like shit. Can you still run?" Lisa asked.

"Well, LIIIISA, given the choice of being left in Terra Alta to be eaten alive, or running for my life, I'll take running for my life. So, move along, don't worry about the *old man*," I retorted while bent over catching my breath. Lisa shook her head, turned on her heel and took off at a sprint.

Randy came up beside me and said, "You can't run, can you?"

I looked up and said, "Not a chance, Randy. I might die in Terra Alta. Go on, save yourself."

"You're so dramatic, Otto. You getting ready for Hollywood?" he replied and then continued, "Know this, you don't figure out a way to run, Lisa will hold it over your head forever. Now, you may die and not have to listen to her trash-talk you. But that just means she'll trash-talk you at your funeral."

I suddenly felt better, like I could run a marathon. "Randy, give me some tape from your bag. I'll fix this boot old-school."

I taped my boot together in a flash then took off after the group. In the time I'd spent fixing my boot, they had put about fifty yards between us. The UC herd hit the razor-wire immediately after I began running towards the team. Razor wire is good at stopping living beings; it merely slowed down dead ones. Thankfully, that's all I needed. Even as beat up as I was, I should be able to move faster than the herd. If I kept them behind me, that is.

After running several hundred yards that seemed more like six miles on sand, I saw Randy reach the Hummer.

I sensed the herd behind me and risked a look over my shoulder. "We have company, people," I yelled to the team.

The main UC herd hadn't made up much ground on me. However, roughly twenty UCs had joined the chase at some point. The ripped clothing and shredded skin identified them as *barrier crashers*. I just didn't know at what point we'd picked them up and it wasn't important, I needed to get to the Hummer ASAP.

Lisa screamed, "Down in front!" as she shouldered her Sig MPX carbine (I swear she aimed at my head). I hit the ground a second before she opened fire on the approaching UCs. Twenty-two shots later, twenty UCs lay dead on the road behind me. I bolted for the Hummer as she dropped the empty mag and loaded another.

As I approached the Hummer, I realized it wasn't running. Randy's expression, visible through the windshield, told me something was wrong. "In, get in now," he yelled.

While I raced to the front passenger door, I heard the engine struggling to turn over. It was not playing nice with Randy, and his frustration was evident. When I got situated in the Hummer, I saw why Randy was freaking out. More UC monsters were exiting the house we had used to get past the roadblock just a few hours before. It became obvious we hadn't secured it when we exited and the UCs had found their way through. If we didn't get moving, we would be surrounded by a herd of monsters too large to push through.

"Randy, this feels like the final scene in a B-Movie. The kind of movie where all the passengers die. Please don't make us the stars of that movie!" I yelled as Randy gave it another try. Finally, the engine roared to life.

With crazy-eyes burning bright, he yelled, "Hold on, it's about to get bumpy."

Randy slammed his foot on the accelerator as the first of the UCs reached the passenger side of the Hummer. He cut hard to the right, plowing into the UC and hurling it out of the way. Something about the UC was unsettling. It appeared to reach for the recessed door handle just before being hit by the Hummer. I hoped it was a coincidence, but it also lined up with what had happened at Stone's community. We really didn't need them developing functional motor skills. If they did, I'd never sleep again.

The tight turning radius of the Hummer allowed Randy to miss most of the herd. Most, not all. The brush-guard clipped the leading edge of the herd with a deafening thud. The UCs scattered like bowling pins. All except one. The lone UC became entangled in the brush-guard. Its badly decomposed head was barely visible over the hood. With spoiled-milk eyes it stared, hungrily, at the cab full of food.

Stone poked his head between the seats and said, "That thing is making me mad. Can you shake it lose? I can't have it staring at me the whole way home."

As if on cue, Randy hit a large rut and the UC flipped into the air. Its left arm didn't budge as the rest of its body traveled over the hood, detaching it from the UC. What remained of the monster came down hard on the hood, leaving a gooey mess behind as it slid off the Hummer and landed in a broken heap as we continued our escape. We agreed that the UC arm, flapping in the brush-guard, was far more acceptable than the thing's face.

Chapter 12
The Threat

"Un-ac-ceptable, Mr. Williams. Completely and utterly unacceptable. You failed, Soldier-boy. We have no tug-fleet left. You and your ragtag group of hangers-on failed." The senator raged from the comfort of that chair of his. "How could you let this happen, how? Tell me, HOW?"

Williams hadn't bothered to stand at attention when he entered Senator Shafter's office. He watched, detached from the scene, as spittle flew from the senator's mouth during his tirade. In his mind's eye, he imagined himself removing the senator's larynx from his scrawny neck, barehanded, of course.

"Do I amuse you, Mr. Williams?"

The question caught Williams off guard. Then he realized he was smiling. "No, Senator, you're not amusing. I was distracted thinking about something more enjoyable than listening to you blather on."

"Well, Soldier-boy, I'm happy for you. You're the only person on the planet that can find a reason to smile. Maybe you haven't been paying attention to the goings-on in the world."

Williams lurched forward, stopping himself an inch from the senator's desk. The senator, instinctively, pushed back from his desk, but never left that damn chair.

"Listen up, you cowardly prick, the only reason you're not dead is because I took an oath. Unlike you, giving my word means something," Williams said as he leaned over the senator's desk.

"Men, civilian men, lost their lives today, for nothing more than your lust for power. So, I'm fully aware of the *goings-on*. I get to tell the families that *you* killed their loved ones."

Williams straightened and adjusted his black ACU with a sharp downward-tug. He found the senator's eyes and locked on them before he continued, "The rest of your plan has been implemented. The resources we had in place on RAM soil are attacking the outposts of RAM civilians. We've lost eight *boys* to date. Remember what I told you? Figure out the eight body parts you can live without. I'll be back to collect them when your *mission* is over."

The senator used the heels of his feet to pull himself back to his desk. Williams had come to hate that frigging chair. The senator treated it as a throne, rarely leaving it. Suspicion grabbing hold of his thoughts, he decided he needed to know why.

"Mr. Williams, you should also try to remember what I told you. You're a lackey for those of us in power. Like it or not, I'm the only power holding this side of the BSU together. If you don't care to continue to live in this safe zone, I can arrange to end the relationship."

The veiled threat didn't get past Williams, but he didn't tip his hand. "I'll sleep on your offer, Senator. Anything else? Because I'm trying to keep the walls of your *safe zone* from being breached and need to rally the lackeys to do so."

The senator waved Williams off. As he left the room, the senator called after him, "Have extra rations delivered to the families of the people killed. That should be ample compensation for their losses."

Williams gritted out his response: "You. Are. An. Ass. Sleep well tonight."

He slammed the door behind him and addressed the guard in the hall. "I want to be notified the second the senator leaves his office for the night. Do not share that order with a single person. Have I been clear?"

"Yes sir, very clear sir," the young soldier responded.

After Williams exited, the senator gave a silent ten-count before tapping the secret compartment on the seat of his chair. He removed a single piece of paper and secured the compartment. Grabbing his desk key, he unlocked the bottom drawer and removed the satellite phone. With a slight tremor, he dialed the number on the paper and waited. When his call was answered, he said, "Speak English when I call you."

Chapter 13
It's Going To Be A Long Ride

"Please tell me you're joking, Jackson! What the hell do we do now?" Natalia said. Jack simply stared at her. "Say something. Do something. Blink, blinking would be a good start because that unblinking stare is freaking me out."

Jack managed to blink, just once. In the light filtering in from the garage's transom windows, his face remained motionless.

"Jackson, I'm not going to die in this garage. Are you clear on that?"

Jack woke from his stupor and press-checked his M&P, again, and moved towards the door. "Natalia, get in the truck. I'm going to get the keys."

Natalia, suddenly not sure if this was the action she wanted Jackson to take, started to object. "Jacks—"

He cut her off. "Now, Natalia, get in the truck now. Time's not our friend. We need those keys."

Worry straining her features, she conceded the point and climbed into the large Ford F250.

Jack turned back to the door, currently under assault by at least one UC, and took a deep breath. *This is going to suck*, he thought as he aimed his gun about head height for an average person. The thunderous shot in the small confines sent razorblades through his ears. Normal sound was replaced with a high-pitched ringing. It was impossible to hear if his action had the desired results. He placed a hand on the door. It wasn't moving; the UC assault had stopped.

Ears still useless, Jack pushed hard against the door. The gamble paid off and the dead UC now blocked the door. After a straining heave, Jack was able to squeeze through the door and stand next to the dead UC. The bullet had entered its skull at the crown of its head. Half an inch higher and it would be eating him right now. The path the bullet followed carved a gruesome part down the center of its head. Like a freakish '80s feathered hairdo.

Jack bolted for the keys hanging a mere three feet away. His right foot seemed to freeze mid-step, sending him to the floor and slamming his head onto the tile with a resounding thud. His vision went hazy as he struggled to remain conscious. Something brushed against his back. An instant later he noticed movement near the key-hook. His hearing and vision impaired, Jack launched into a full-blown panic. "Nooo, this isn't how it ends for us," he screamed, pushing himself to his knees. "I will not die on the floor! Get ready to meet your maker, you freak." Jack raised his gun to end the monster.

"Meet your maker? Did you really just say that? What are you, twelve?" Was that Natalia's voice he heard over the ringing, not a monster's rasp responding to his valiant proclamation? And, of course, busting his balls.

"Your foot is tangled in the monster's armpit, and it happened because you don't pay attention. Stand up! Our house is buzzing with UCs and we're still technically trapped in the garage. I'll let you save us from that situation. Sound good?"

Natalia helped him to his feet and they exited the house without looking back. The door began to rattle in its frame as they ran to the truck.

"Get in the driver's seat!" Jack yelled. "I've got to pull the release cord then open the door manually." He worked his way to the garage entrance to check for sound. A slight ringing was all he heard. "Damn it, I should have listened to Stone and bought the ear protection." He cursed.

"Jackson, what if they're waiting for you? What if you don't move fast enough? What if I freeze?"

Jack looked at her and said, "You sound like Otto. Don't *what if* this to death. I'm going to pull the emergency release cord, the door will retract about a foot, then I'll run to the door and throw it open. At that very second, you hit the gas."

"What if—"

Jack spoke over his wife. "No time! The door from the house won't hold much longer. When the door opens, stand on the gas." Not waiting for a response, he grabbed the cord and pulled. Light flooded into the garage, casting shadows across the floor. Jack hesitated as he approached the door. *Maybe this wasn't the best idea… or maybe this isn't the best time to second-guess yourself. MOVE.* He reached down with one hand and heaved the door open. He didn't hang around to see if any UCs stood in their path to freedom; instead, he ran to the truck as Natalia floored the gas-pedal. As the truck lurched forward, Jack gripped the door handle and was pulled forward. Feet scraping along the ground, he screamed, "WHAT ARE YOU DOING? Stop the damn truck!"

The truck tires screeched as it halted its forward progress. Jack climbed in, slamming the door shut just as a UC he hadn't noticed banged against the window. Natalia again jammed the accelerator to the floor while Jack glared at her. The truck fishtailed as it exited the garage and Natalia steered it left down the driveway.

The large UC crowd had mostly congregated at the front of the house where Jack had first spotted them. They were pouring into their home through shattered windows, searching for the food that had just escaped them. Natalia took a hard left at the end of the drive. The truck shuddered as its wheels struggled for purchase on the blacktop.

After bringing the large F250 under control, Natalia screamed as a UC wearing a sundress covered in filth and blood shuffled into their path. The monster looked up as if it realized food was close, exposing its horrible face to them. Its nose was missing and the skin around its nasal cavity had been peeled back like a banana, yet its hungry gaze locked onto them. It raised its claw-like hands in their direction. Natalia let loose a rollercoaster yell as the truck sped towards the hungry UC and slammed it to the blacktop.

"Woooo, BAM! Try it again, bitch, same thing's gonna happen to your ugly ass." The truck bounced as it rolled over the now severely mangled UC.

Jack stared at his wife with awe and fear. "I don't even know who you are anymore," he said as they careened down the narrow rural road.

With her face alight and all of her teeth showing in an ear to ear grin, she yelled, "I'm a survivor, bitches."

Natalia spotted another monster heading for the road and gripped the steering wheel tight in anticipation of scoring another kill.

"NATALIA, STOP!"

Tires kicking up gravel, the truck slid to a stop. "What, what do you see, Jackson?"

He responded, "I see the same thing as you, only I want to avoid it. We need the truck to get us to Otto's community. You keep slamming into these *bitches* and we won't make it to the damn freeway."

After a full minute, Natalia finally spoke. "That was a frigging rush."

A little worried about his wife's mental state, Jack asked, "Were you going to leave me in the garage? You were, weren't you; just leave me to die on the cold, oil-stained floor."

She shot him a hard look. "No, I did what you told me to do, Jackson Hammer. Let me refresh your memory—"

Jack spoke up quickly. "I know what I said, but at some point I figured you'd stop."

Eyes rolling, she said, "At some point I figured you had a stupid plan to get in the truck. Now, can I drive again? That thing is getting close and I wouldn't want it to scratch up your precious truck."

Jack took a long slow breath, realizing it was going to be a long ride. "Yes, please just drive."

Chapter 14
The Breach

The explosion punched a hole in the fencing roughly fifty feet from the main gate. Dillan's first thought was *Thank God for the jersey-barriers.* Without them, the UCs would have unfettered access to the community. As it were, several UC had already slimed their way through the small breach. Dillan saw Darline and Kit converging on the scene from the west as he advanced from the east. He noticed that Kit only carried an aluminum baseball bat, and the revelation startled him. Darline, gripping a 9mm Steyr L-A1, had already opened fire on the UCs that remained in the street. Her fire joined that of the guards already on scene.

Other members of the community began joining the fight. A burst of adrenaline pushed him faster towards the breach. As he neared the battle, one member stood out. It was Kit; she had pinned a UC against a tree and was pummeling it.

Swinging the bat back and forth, she screamed a word with each stroke. "YOU." *clang* "WILL." *thwack* "NOT." *clang* "TAKE." *thwack* "THIS." *clang* "FROM." *thwack* "US." *clang*.

Darline moved in behind Kit to cover her while she was preoccupied exacting a little revenge. "Kit, I love what you're doing, but I need a little help. Can you pick out another UC to beat into submission?"

Kit immediately turned, aluminum bat locked in her right hand, and re-entered the fray.

Darline moved forward with the other gunners to avoid friendly fire on those fighting with sharp and blunt-edged weapons. She heard Kit's continuous narration as she assaulted the UCs that made it past the firing line. Darline fell into a hypnotic rhythm: aim, shoot, and repeat. Her body count was piling up.

Suddenly, she was on the ground, hit hard from her left side, "I will kill you, you stinking pus-bag. How dare you TOUCH me! Show me your head, you pus-bag, come on, show it to me!" she screamed while struggling to right herself, fists swinging wildly as she pumped her legs in her efforts to break free of the monster's grasp.

"Darline, don't shoot me, and stop punching me!" Dillan's voice broke through the haze of Darline's one-sided battle.

"What in the holy hell are you doing? We are in a fig—." Her words caught in her throat when Dillan rolled off and shot the UC stalking her from behind. After getting a look at the twice-dead UC, she thought, *You really were a pus-bag.* Dillan's shot entered the monster through the nose. The entry wound now leaked grayish-green pus. The UC wore a Gucci leather belt with a Gucci scarf cinched like a noose around its neck. *You, dear, are not from our neighborhood.* The realization caused her stress level to skyrocket. "I'll be back for the belt, pus-bag," she said as she got back to her feet. "Thanks, Dillan." Then she picked out her next target.

The UC crowd had been thinned out considerably on both sides of the fence. The hand-to-hand combat ceased and those with handheld weapons formed up behind the firing line ready to intercept any UC that broke through. When the slide on her Steyr locked back, she retreated to reload when she heard an engine roaring as it accelerated closer to the breech. Panic set in as the group struggled to identify the intention of the now visible pickup truck. She slammed the magazine into the mag-well and released the slide, chambering a round. She adjusted her position and lined up the truck's windshield. As she increased the force on the gun's five-pound trigger, a head popped from the passenger window.

"Hold your fire, hold your fire!" Darline yelled to the others as they too took aim at the truck. Assuming it was a threat, each and every gun on the line had been pointed at the truck as it sped in their direction.

The truck made contact with four or five UCs, their bodies crumpling under the force of the extra-large vehicle. Then it course-corrected toward the breach in the fence. A familiar voice, making an unfamiliar sound, came from the truck as the driver's window powered down.

Chapter 15
Forfeiture

The drive on Brandonville Pike Road had been quiet.

"What did Jax mean when he said *Be The Storm?*" Lisa asked.

"*Satan whispered to the warrior, you cannot withstand the storm. The warrior whispered back, I am the storm,*" Stone answered. "It was tattooed on his back. He told me he got the tattoo while going through the darkest period of his life. A time when he almost gave up. He said he woke up one day, his soul battered by life's trials, and read it on the back of a magazine. He decided to fight. At that moment, he decided to fight."

The cab fell quiet after Stone finished speaking, all of us replaying the day's events in our minds. Our friend was dead because two people that had entered RAM without permission didn't know how to fight and pulled us away from our home.

When we turned onto Route 5, our non-military two-way radio squawked to life with heavy interference and a voice said, "Hazelton TOC for MST1, how copy?"

Will grabbed it and, depressing the talk button, said, "MST1, good copy."

"MST1 Camp Hazelton, Tactical Operation Command requests a sit-rep, over."

After a long pause, Will said, "MST1 encountered two survivors; neither were RAM citizens. We also encountered hundreds of UCs. Terra Alta is a loss and will need to be sanitized—"

The voice from Hazelton TOC cut in, "MST1, what's the sit-rep on survivors? Over."

"The BSU survivors are a negative." After breathing out slowly, Will continued, "MST1 lost one good man today, in case you were ever going to get around to asking for a sit-rep on our team."

The voice from the Hazelton TOC filled the cab. "MST1, did you take direct-fire from enemy-combatants, over?"

"Hazelton, affirmative on the enemy fire. Both combatants were neutralized, over."

"Why did you allow the survivors to b—"

Will screamed into the radio, "Hazelton, you sent MST1 into a shit-storm with bad INTEL and lack of support. We lost a member of our team today. He sacrificed his life for us. Our position was overrun by the hundreds of UC YOU failed to identify—"

Hazelton TOC cut Will off again, "MST1, the world is falling apart, and we are killing thousands of civilians every day. We have lost hundreds of brave men and women to the virus. That's the reality of our new world. Your friend's forfeiture, although brave, is but a drop in the bucket in the lives that have been lost. Over."

My hand was on the radio before my mind registered what it was doing. I began addressing the Hazelton TOC an instant later. "Hazelton, this is Team Lead Otto Hammer. The difference between forfeiture and sacrifice is significant. Forfeiture implies that Jax didn't show up for the fight, something a coward sitting in a secured facility would do. You may be more familiar with that action. Sacrifice describes Jax's last act as a warrior. It describes what someone does when they place value on the lives around them, not just their own life. Hazelton, you need to listen to me very closely… Fuck YOU!" I threw the radio to the floorboard while my brain raged. Jax shouldn't be dead; we should be protecting our community, not the wall. And if that idiot in the Hazelton TOC spewed any more gibberish, I would find him and dot both of his eyes.

The radio squawked to life again, "MST1, this is Hazelton TOC. How copy? Over." We left the radio on the floorboard. With a more forceful tone, the voice hailed us again, "MST1, this is Camp Hazelton, TOC. How copy? Over."

Not wanting to hear the voice for the entire journey back to Hazelton, I picked it up and said, "Hazelton, MST1 good copy, over."

The voice, that I now hated, said, "MST1, please identify your K.I.A."

I held the radio to my mouth and paused. Looking the question at Randy, he shot me a hard look when he realized what the question was. "Cunningham," he said. "Jax Cunningham."

The inside of the cab bristled at the realization that I had no idea what Jax's full name was. Before they could begin to assault me and my shortcomings, I answered the voice from the Hazelton TOC. "Jax Cunningham. His name is Jax Cunningham."

"Will his family need to be notified?"

I knew the answer to this question and said, "None we are aware of. He lived alone in our community. And we would do it ourselves if it needed to be done."

The most annoying voice in the history of time said, "Master Sergeant Lucas orders you to report directly to her post upon your arrival at Camp Hazelton."

Something in my brain did a back-flip at the mention of the Master Sergeant. My right eye twitched and a vein in my forehead pulsed while my lips curled into a sideways lunatic-grin.

"Tell the Master Sergeant to bite me. We don't take orders from her, or any of you for that matter. Advise Lucas we'll be bypassing Camp Hazelton. We are going home to protect our community. Also, tell her she really isn't a nice person. And she needs to use Visine on those eyes of hers. MST1 out. Yes, I mean OUT, not OVER, this conversation is over, damn it, I mean it's done." I turned the radio off and again threw it to the floorboard.

Randy broke the silence when he said, "Otto, how is it possible that you didn't know Jax's last name?"

I was hoping the team had forgotten my *miscue*. I shot back, "Randy, I knew his last name. The heat of the moment threw me. Just the heat of the moment."

"Ah," Randy started. "Just the heat of the moment. Got it. Perfectly understandable. So, Otto, tell me, what's my last name?"

"Really, Randy? You're asking me that question now, somehow trying to make this about you? How very *center of the universe* of you, Randy."

Randy shook his head and asked again, "Otto, what's my last name?"

I was in deep with no lifeline, so I blurted out, "Well, Randy that's an easy one. It's Daywalker. You happy now? Can we get back to the business of getting home?"

Randy, with face in palm, said, "Dayal, Otto, my last name is Dayal."

My face felt hot and the tips of my ears burned with a mix of embarrassment and anger. "Well, Randy. Maybe if you didn't spend so much time not talking to me, I'd have a reason to use your last name more. And, in turn, would remember it."

Before Randy was able to reply, Lisa said, "Otto, what's my last name?"

Not a chance I remembered her last name. She was lucky I cared enough to remember her first name. Actually, I didn't care that much. She was just around a lot because she and Darline were friends so I had no choice.

"You know what, Lisa? You damn near shot me in the head. Then used twenty-two bullets to kill twenty slow-moving UCs. So, your name isn't all that important to me." I was flailing again, grasping at anything to save face. "Will, before you even ask, your last name is Noting. It's easy because when we met, I said *Will is Noting going to borrow my tools*. It's called word association."

Then Lisa said, "Maybe you ought to pay more attention. Because, Otto, you inevitably sound like a jerk." She flicked, yes actually flicked, the back of my head as she finished spouting off.

I openly admit that I can be a bit of a jerk. Mostly, it's a personality defect. I usually don't get to people's last names in a conversation. When I do, I often forget them. It's not that the person isn't important; it's just that I usually don't care enough to commit them to memory. I have a lot going on in this brain of mine and last names just take up space.

In an attempt to bring us back to the task at hand, and get them off my back, I said, "Has anyone figured out how to bypass Camp Hazelton?" That question shut them all up. Game, set, and match!

Chapter 16
Worm

"No. I won't call him Dear Leader," the senator said, holding tightly to the thin shreds of his patience that remained. "Once again, speak English and no, I will not call him Dear Leader. Put the arrogant fat toad on the phone, NOW. I enjoy precious little time and he's wasting it while trying to exert power he no longer possesses."

The heavily accented, supremely smug voice on the other side of the world said, "*Senator Shafter, Dear Leader is very busy man. He has no time to talk to tiny, slime-covered worms. The worms that no longer hold power of planet. Dear Leader will visit soon, take everything from imperial scum and crush all the worms under his mighty feet of power.*"

Senator Shafter, face burning bright, and not convinced the other man's English made him easier to understand, responded, "Look, you little shit-ball. You idiots managed to destroy the world. You assured me, and the other leaders on the Coalition to Reunite America Permanently, that the DPRK could control this monster. HOW WILL YOU FIX THIS?" As he waited for a response, Shafter realized he was talking to dead air. The DPRK representative had disconnected.

He jabbed his finger on the end-call button of the Iridium Extreme Satellite Phone, not receiving the satisfaction one gets when they slam the receiver down on an old-school desk phone. He decided to slam it onto his desk. Shafter leaned back and while staring at the aging and stained ceiling-tiles said, "Well, it would appear we opened a second front in this *war*. History doesn't smile on two-front wars, nor the people that launch them." As he finished his one-sided conversation, the lights flickered and went dark and the emergency siren began to wail.

Chapter 17
Welcome To Camp Hopkins

Chief Warrant Officer Albright had run out of patience. "Riggins, answer the question. Answer the question now. If you choose not to, we'll arrange to have you delivered back to your boat."

Riggins glanced at John, who was as puzzled as Albright. The captain hadn't shared his plan with John before they were taken aboard the RAM Black Hawk and brought to Camp Hopkins.

"Remove the restraints and I'll answer your questions," the captain said.

"That's enough," Albright barked. "Stand and face the wall. We'll be moving out in fifteen. You will not be given life jackets for your return to your boat."

Riggins stood and locked Albright in a burning glare and said, "It's a tugboat, not simply a boat. Don't you operate with any form of *military code of honor* or some such nonsense? Some *moral code* that prohibits you from executing civilians?"

Albright removed his K-Bar 1213 from its nylon sheath and had it to Riggins' throat within a second. Returning the captain's glare, Albright said, "You stopped being civilians the moment you agreed to bring death to RAM's shores. You, sir, are an enemy combatant and we are at war. RAM doesn't possess the resources to hold POWs. I will be doing my country a favor when I launch your worthless carcass into the lake. Or, I could save our fuel by ending you right here."

A drop of blood trickled down Riggins' neck as the tip of Albright's K-Bar found its way past his epidermis on its way to his jugular. The look in Albright's eyes showed a warrior preparing to claim the head of his enemy. As the pressure increased, Riggins relented.

"Chief Warrant Officer Albright, you have persuaded me to talk. Bring me a map and I'll show you the exact point of our tugs' embarkation."

John had been watching the drama unfold and began to rationalize his death at the hands of the RAM soldier. When Albright removed the large knife from the captain's neck, he exhaled the breath he had no idea he was holding. "Thank you, Captain. I thought we were going to die today."

The captain glanced over his shoulder and said, "The day is young, John. We have no guarantee at life past the moment we live in."

Albright spoke into his shoulder-mounted radio, "Sergeant Willis, this is Chief Warrant Officer Albright, over."

Albright's radio squawked as a voice replied, "Go for Willis, over."

"Sergeant Willis, you and your men will report to Terminal C, security room A4. And Willis, arrive combat ready, out."

Willis immediately responded with, "Always, sir. Reporting to your location in five, out."

Albright turned his attention to Riggins and John and said, "John, your captain has never spoken truer words. Now, Mr. Riggins, show me the location of your embarkation on the map. And understand this, if your information isn't truthful, it will be your last act as a living being."

Albright then leaned in close to Captain Riggins and whispered, "I lost my family yesterday, every member of my family. Their community fell to over a thousand UCs. When we sanitized the area, all of them carried out-of-state IDs. If you're a religious man, you best pray we find this *depot* you speak of."

Chapter
18 Mop It Up

"Nat, what are you doing here? What happened to your house?" Darline asked Natalia while scanning the inside of the truck cab looking for Jackson. Not seeing him, she said, "Nat, where's Jack?" Her voice rattled with stress and worry.

"I'm here, Darline. No worries," Jack said from somewhere in the backseat.

Natalia, in full-blown eye roll said, "He got a little excited when he figured out what I was about to do."

Jack's head appeared from behind the front seat. Eyes wild and hair equally untamed, he said, "A little excited? That's what you call it? Look, my heart may have stopped during that stunt of yours. My entire life passed in front of my closed eyes."

Darline went to her tip-toes and said, "So, is that why you're in the backseat? Trying to find a comfortable place to have a heart attack?"

Jack looked a question at her, and Darline said, "You're in the backseat. You said your heart was going to stop. That's a heart attack, Jackson."

"Oh, for God's sake, I know what a heart attack is. Did you and my wife go to the same school of smartassery?" He paused and looked out the window at the few remaining UCs walking towards the truck. "I'm just not sure how I ended up in the backseat. The last thing I remember was Natalia, *The Goddess of War*, letting loose a feral scream and punching the accelerator.

After that it's all a hazy mess of fast-moving trees, an odd view of the truck's backseat, and an incredibly loud thud." He looked over at Natalia and said, "Cover your Goddess-sized ears, dear." Jack had the window down and fired six shots before Natalia could even ask why. The last four UC were put down by Jack's assault.

"Jack, did it actually take you six shots to kill those UCs?"

Jack beamed with pride and said, "Why yes, yes it only took six shots."

With a slight shake of her head, Darline responded, "Okay, we'll work on your shooting now that you'll be living in our community."

Natalia, obviously amused, added," Yeah, Jackson, get to work on your shooting. We require four shots, four kills."

Jack shook off the insult and asked, "Darline, where are my brothers? The last I talked to them, they said they were training with the military to become a support team, or something. Are they okay?"

"Nat, follow me to the gate, and I'll fill you both in on everything."

Darline turned to let Kit know that Natalia and Jack had arrived only to find her walking to each of the fallen UC and applying several additional *whacks* to their heads. Her gaze drifting from Kit, the scale of the carnage revealed itself. Two dozen UCs lay dead behind the fence while dozens more lay twisted in the street outside the community. Several residents of the community appeared to be injured from the blast. Durrell tended to the most serious of the injured while Dillan and Al performed basic first-aid on the others. Windows in several homes nearest the blast had been blown out. It appeared that every citizen of the community was present and helping in some way. They had no protocol for this, no real plan of action for what to do when attacked by a hostile force of the living variety. Darline told Natalia and Jack to hold tight and ran to Dillan. "What do we do?"

Dillan, who just finished applying a dressing to Sam Houston's arm, stood and said, "Tell your friends in the truck not to move. They have the breach blocked and that'll help stop any straggling UCs from entering. Get them a couple of guns so they can defend themselves, but don't let them move that truck."

Darline threw her arms around Dillan and said, "Thank you for saving my life." Then bolted back to the truck and handed her gun and several loaded magazines to Natalia. "Don't move from this position, and shoot any monsters coming in this direction. We clear on that?"

"Crystal," Jack said, "what happened? This isn't as simple as a breach in your fence. It looks deliberate, it looks planned, and it feels like we'll need to take our pound of flesh from someone."

Nodding, Darline turned away from the truck. She now saw the big picture. The community had been attacked; it was an act of war. But why them? Why attack civilians? Turning on other living beings while the world was eating itself alive played like one of Otto's zombie books. "Note to self, ask Otto how this story ends," she said while rushing to help with the wounded.

Running into Durrell, quite literally, she asked him, "How can I help?"

Durrell didn't respond. He was staring, fixated, in the direction of the quarantine homes. Following his gaze, the reason for his distraction became clear. Andy and his wife were standing outside of the quarantine area, breathing heavily. Both held bloody lawn tools they had used as bludgeoning weapons. Several UC lay crumpled at their feet.

Andy noticed he was drawing the attention of several residents, including Darline and Durrell, so he said, "Don't worry. I haven't eaten anyone, and I feel no urge to eat humans. Well, maybe I'll eat Durrell, but only him."

Durrell turned sharply to Darline and said, "I told you he's a little jerk. I'm not even sure how the little man kept his wife. Jerk." Turning back to Andy, he yelled, "Still a little jerk, that's what you are, a little jerk."

Durrell went back to work on the wounded while Andy's toothy smile told Darline he'd achieved the reaction he sought from Durrell. He then made a waving motion, calling her over.

Darline started in Andy's direction when she was intercepted by Randy's wife, Nila. Her hands were stained with blood and her eyes empty of emotion. She asked Darline to help calm a young man, of maybe fifteen years, whose name Darline didn't know, but whose face was familiar. Nila was attempting to apply a dressing to a large gash on his right arm. The fear in his eyes kicked Darline's maternal instincts into high gear.

Brushing back his sweat-soaked hair, she asked, "What's your name, sweetie?

Eyes screwed shut from the pain of the dressing being applied, the young man said, "Charlie, Charlie Biggs, ma'am."

"Listen to you, manners still top of mind. You can call me Darline." Then she asked, "What happened to you, Charlie?"

With the dressing fully applied, Charlie seemed a little more relaxed. He said, "Miss Darline, I was helping fortify the southwest corner of the fence when I heard the gunfire. The whole crew headed to the gate to see what was happening. We saw the UCs as soon as we rounded the corner. I told Alex we needed to help thin them out, and that's what we started doing. Our knives came out, and we started putting them down through the fence." Charlie paused while he searched his memory, trying to piece the events back together. He locked onto Darline's eyes and said, "One of them exploded! We had put down four of five when one of them, about twenty-feet away, just exploded. Like a terrorist with a suicide vest." His eyes welled with tears as he finished his story. "I couldn't help after that; something hit my arm hard and pushed me to the ground. The world went dark and my ears were ringing. When it all cleared up, Miss Nila was by me with a big smile on her face telling me it was going to be alright. How did it explode? Why did this happen?"

With no answers for the brave young man, Darline simply said, "Charlie, I don't know what happened but I'm sure going to find out."

Nila had been listening intently to his story and broke into the conversation. "Charlie, do you think you can stand?" He nodded. Nila and Darline helped him to his feet. "Can you walk?" He nodded again. "Good, I had a feeling you're a tough one. Now, get to the clinic, tell Sabrina about your wound. Let her know that I put a compression dressing and a clotting agent on your wound."

Charlie nodded and looked over his shoulder at the scene. He returned his gaze to the women and asked, "Why would someone do this to us?" Not waiting for an answer, he headed to the clinic.

When the young man cleared earshot, Darline looked at Nila and said, "What's happening? I'll echo Charlie: Why would someone attack us?"

Nila's answer only compounded Darline's feeling of dread. "Why is any of this happening? A madman wanted so badly to destroy America that he brought the entire world to its knees. Now, the dead don't stay dead, our husbands need to help the most powerful military on the planet, and someone attacked our home. A place that has offered safety and shelter to others. The world is spiraling, and we are the only ones who can stop its descent." Nila paused for a moment, appearing to view something in her mind. "The things I've seen in the homes we've cleaned and sterilized will be with me until I'm buried. We need to stop this."

Nila had been directing the abandoned/infected home cleanup crew. She hadn't been able to break away to do much else but scrub blood and dispose of body parts since this started. She was perfectly suited for the job as she managed a small cleaning company that had a crime scene restoration division. But the enormity of the job coupled with the realization she was cleaning up the remains of friends and neighbors was pulling her under.

Andy yelled to Darline, directing her back to her original task. "Darline, do you have a minute? It has to do with the attack."

Nila said, "Go ahead. It looks like we are getting things under control. But I have a couple of questions. What's he doing outside the quarantine zone and, more importantly, why does he now look like a swimsuit model?"

Darline chuckled at the swimsuit comment and said, "I was thinking the same thing. He sure didn't look like that when he entered quarantine. I'll catch up with you later." She hugged her friend goodbye and headed towards Andy.

"Mr. Wilms, you don't seem to be making friends with Durrell. Do you think that's a wise move? He and Sabrina are the closest things we have to doctors and seeing we no longer have a system to deal with malpractice, you may find yourself with a thermometer wedged permanently in your ear… or worse."

Andy, with his toothy smile lingering on his face, said, "Darline, I just can't help myself. He makes it too easy."

"He really does, doesn't he? He was an unsteady mess when he came to Pat and me about your family moving in with you."

Andy, smile departing his face, said, "Thanks for letting that happen. My life's much better since they've joined me. But I didn't call you over for that. I saw what happened with the exploding UC. It literally just exploded; I was watching from the bedroom window. The exploder was a straggler. I was watching to see if others were following him. He detonated about twenty feet from the fence. Thank God for that. Any closer and the fence would have been destroyed and granted the UCs unrestricted access to the community. Another stroke of luck is he took out a good twenty UCs in the herd. I doubt any of the gunfire set him off; I'm guessing he was on a timer. The fire was concentrated on the UCs at the fence. He came in behind the main group completely untouched."

Darline chewed on that information for a minute before responding, "We're going to have to expand our perimeter. This cannot happen again." As a thought struck her, she cocked her head and asked, "How did you and Janet *escape* quarantine?" She shifted her gaze to Janet and said, "Hello, Mrs. Wilms," and hugged her long-time friend.

"It was lunch time, and our food service had just shown up. When the gunfire started, the guard dropped the food and headed for the fence. In his rush, he forgot to lock us up. Don't tell Dillan, I don't want to get the guard in any trouble. But we couldn't just stand by as those things walked into our home. We set up our own little *perimeter* and picked off the few that made it this far. Quarantine or not, this is our home, and no one is going to take it from us."

Darline nodded in agreement; this community was worth fighting for and this attack had only solidified her dedication to it. Pulling them into a group hug, she said, "Thank you both. We need people like you. Now, please get back in quarantine before Dillan sees you and has an aneurism."

She noticed Andy was still an odd color and his eyes still appeared hazy, but he looked healthy. His grip was firm, his mind sharp, and since Janet and the kids moved in with him, his emotional state had become rock solid. They needed to make a decision about him returning to the community, and soon. They needed him.

Turning from her friends, she called out "Dillan, let's mop this up; we have an expansion in our future!"

Chapter 19
Open Fire

The guards on the raised platforms had been trying to provide cover for the desperate throngs seeking safety inside RAM's borders. Their arms began cramping from the unending streams of fire they unleashed on the UC that relentlessly assaulted the bewildered survivors. The Entry Point gate was ordered sealed at eleven hundred hours. They sealed the holding area outside the gate at twelve hundred hours.

The order came as a crush of humanity overran the area causing the Entry Point gate's massive v-grooved rollers to become jammed by living bodies on its tracks. Ground troops inside the gate nearly opened fire into the masses of living, but avoided doing so when the gate was finally forced over the limbs and torsos impeding its progress.

The scene was ghastly as arms and legs flopped to the ground, spraying blood along the pavement and bottom of the gate as it locked shut. The action caused the troops to become hyper-vigilant and a little less selective with their covering fire. Living and UC alike were caught in the hailstorm of bullets raining down from the platforms.

That had been over three hours ago and the crush of people still trying to enter RAM extended past the platforms for miles.

Apaches and Black Hawks had navigated further into BSU trying to cut the dead down before they reached the survivors at the gate. The Apache's 30mm Chain-guns, working in unison with the Black Hawk's M134 Gatling-guns, brought devastation to the ranks of UC seeking an easy meal. But the battle was slipping away from them; their guns started overheating and the Apache's Hydra Rocket pods had run dry hours ago.

The spotter on the North Platform attempted to direct the fire of both the copters and soldiers manning the other platforms. Images of the dead feasting on the living filled the glass of the AN/PED-1 Lightweight Laser Designator Rangefinder (LLDR). The spotter panned the LLDR to the south, landing on a heavily decayed UC. The sight caused his breath to hitch. He pulled away from the glass and wiped at his eyes; he had to be seeing things. With his eyes back to the glass, he again found the UC that caused his angst.

The UC shuffled on worn-out shoes as his threadbare full-length overcoat flapped back-and-forth in rhythm with his stride. Underneath the coat and tied around its neck was a piece of cardboard with a crudely written message on it: **Homeless Please Help. God Bless.**

Panning north and south, he saw thousands of the overcoat-wearing UC's traveling companions coming into view.

"Hazelton TOC, this is North Platform. How copy?" The young man anxiously awaited the TOC's confirmation.

"North Platform, this is Hazelton TOC. Good copy."

The soldier nearly cut the TOC off when responding, "We have homeless UC approaching the gate. I repeat, homeless UC approaching the gate. Awaiting orders."

The painfully long pause was broken by the stern voice of Colonel Watts. The colonel said, "Son, relay your confidence level with the INTEL you communicated."

Glancing at the radio with an incredulous expression, the soldier answered, "Message is confirmed, Sir. Patient zeros have reached Entry Point One. Awaiting orders."

The Colonel said, "EVAC your platform via the catwalk."

A moment later, the young soldier listened as a string of orders streamed from his radio. "All personnel cease fire. Platform patrols EVAC your positions immediately, repeat EVAC immediately. All air assets return to Hazelton, repeat all air assets return to Hazelton."

Men and machines moved toward the camp with haste as the orders continued. "All armored units, hold the line at the gate. All artillery-batteries commence bombardment on my command."

The last communication stopped the young soldier in his tracks. With his LLDR slung over his shoulder, he turned to look at the multitude of humanity about to disappear from the planet. It marked an escalation he couldn't fathom. An escalation that, just a few short hours ago, he was confident would never happen. The thought compelled him to move. As he reached the ladder that would take him to safety, the order came.

"This is Colonel Watts. Open fire."

Chapter 20
Straight Shot

"Head east on Centenary Road, it should be coming up on your left. Follow Centenary back to Brandonville Pike, then to 168. That'll put us about eight miles from Camp Hazelton," Stone said from the backseat while reading the map.

That sounded easier than I'd anticipated. They were the first words Stone had uttered since leaving Terra Alta. It was reassuring to hear his voice. We all needed to be home with the people we loved. We needed to allow ourselves to grieve Jax's death. No time for grief now; we had one mission: Get home alive. To achieve that mission, we needed to remain focused.

As we approached the Route 20, Centenary Road split, I noticed a slight shimmy coming from the floorboard. A second later, I felt another, followed by more. The thought that the Hummer might breakdown filled me with dread. I opened my mouth to tell Randy to stop when he slammed on the brakes before I could speak.

Randy asked, "Do you feel that?"

Everyone replied in the affirmative. Curiously, we still felt it after coming to a full four-wheel stop.

"Shut it off," I said. Problem was, Randy had already killed the motor but not the shimmy.

I exited the Hummer. The late afternoon sun to my back afforded me a clear view for miles. Facing east, I should have been able to see the Black Hawk and AH64 Apache air support providing cover to the civilians waiting to enter RAM through Entry Point One. They were nowhere to be found. Instead, the bottoms of the clouds reflected a brilliant orange.

"It's still happening," I said through the open door. A thumping noise in the distance sounded like a heavy metal band's drum solo and the realization of what was happening slapped me in the face. Camp Hazelton had opened up with the Howitzer batteries and pulled the air support back. The tremors those big guns sent through the earth seemed to go on without pause. The gate was under siege. The civilians huddled in the cage and beyond had become indirect victims of the virus. An absolute slaughter was taking place mere miles from our position.

If Camp Hazelton fell, so too would RAM. The UC would flood our country like forty days of rain. No civilian outpost would survive the onslaught.

The others joined me outside the Hummer as the battle for life, just out of sight, stormed on. My bones went cold as visions of a failed Entry Point bounced around my head. Was this happening at all twenty entry points? Had any of them already failed? Willis had told us that they had more UC activity at the west wall. How could it possibly be more than what we had witnessed at Entry Point One? I suddenly felt surrounded and hopelessly exposed. My skin crawled with anxiety as the earth continued to quiver under my feet.

"If it fails, it's over. We all die," Randy said as he watched the clouds reflect the war raging below them.

"This shit's twisting me up, Randy," I said. "We can't build a wall around our home strong enough to stop them if they breach Entry Point One."

Will spoke up, "So, do we contact Camp Hazelton and offer to join the fight? Or do we wish them well and get home to our families? Each choice feels like the wrong choice, if that makes sense. Like we're either abandoning our families or our country. How the hell did we get here?"

"You know we're not that important, right?" Lisa's gregarious voice broke our reverie. "For real, we are only six… I mean five people." She grimaced at her gaffe, but it didn't stop her gums from flapping. "You all need to get over yourselves; we have one choice: Go home. What do you think our poorly trained butts could offer at the Entry Point? Well, besides get in the way of actual War Fighters. Get ourselves killed, that's what." She pulled open the door, locked us in a hard stare, and said, "Let's go, *Big brave men-o-the world*. We need to get home, NOW."

"Loosen your bone, Wilma," I said, sending Lisa into full-tilt. I've never seen a human-being that mad in my life; coming from me, that's a big statement. I've driven people over the edge for years. It's not intentional; I just have a knack for it.

Lisa moved at me like lightning targeting the lone tree in a meadow. She was a blur of movement punctuated with a strike so fast that if my head didn't snap back, I wouldn't have known I'd been battered. Stone and Will grabbed her before she landed a second blow.

"I will KILL you, Otto Hammer. You son-of-a-bitch. How did you even find a wife? That someone hasn't killed you in the street defies logic." She struggled against Will and Stone's restraint and resembled a lunatic being forced into a straitjacket.

"Owww, Lisa, what the hell? You punched me in the face. Hard. Why would you do that?" I said while rubbing my left eye.

The completely unhinged Lisa was stuffed into the backseat of the Hummer while continuing her verbal assault on me. I talked when I should have just kept my mouth shut and said, "Those are some hurtful things you said, WILMA."

"Oh, sounds like you want more of the same, Otto," Lisa yelled, nearly tearing the Hummer's door from its hinges trying to get to me. Her face was so contorted she looked like a Screaming Banshee. She truly scared me. If Will and Stone hadn't blocked her way, I may have retreated, you know, for *her* safety.

Randy grabbed a fistful of my ACU and pulled me out of Lisa's eyeshot. I felt like a child being dragged off the playground by a safety monitor. At about ten feet from the front of the Hummer, he stopped. "Otto, do you have any control over that mouth situated low on your face?" Not sure if he was taking a swipe at my looks or just jabbering out of frustration, I gave him a questioning stare. Apparently, I get under people's skin, and a punch from Randy would hurt a bunch more than from Lisa so I didn't press him when he failed to answer.

A scratchy wet hiss pulled our attention to the field grass where we had just been standing. The sound was unmistakable and demanded action. We noticed the tall, dense grass tremble and split as if a large boa constrictor was slithering towards its next meal. Randy released my ACU and squared up with the movement. He started to remove his Glock 22 RTF from its Kydex holster, then thought better of it. With only one UC approaching, he chose not to waste a bullet. He decided to use his K-Bar 1213 to finish this monster.

As the battle at Camp Hazelton raged on the horizon, Randy approached the slithering grass in a fighting crouch. When the UC became visible through the field grass, Randy launched his attack, bringing the K-Bar down on top of the UC's head and giving it a wiggle for good measure. He removed his blade with a wet sucking noise while rank gray matter seeped from the wound.

As Randy wiped the blade on the monster's shirt, the field grass exploded with movement. It appeared as if a gale-force wind blew through the field in front of Randy's position. Randy gave a startled yelp and fell backwards, trying to shuffle away while on his backside. As he reached the blacktop, four UC stood and began a slow pursuit of the fresh meat on the ground in front of them.

Randy fought to stand as I moved in front of him. My CZ P07 in hand spat death into the heads of the UC ambushers. This crew was clad in heavy denim pants, long-sleeved orange shirts, and leather work gloves. For the time of year, hard-working farmhands possibly explained both their dress and location in the middle of an empty field. The clothes they wore, covered in blood and fresh earth, bore the markings of a violent struggle for life.

The wounds that infected them resided on their faces and necks and oozed a horrible pus-like substance the consistency of rice pudding. Four shots, four kills. I hoped Lisa was paying attention to how it was done. Not a single round went into the field or fell harmlessly to the dirt. No, I had FOUR SHOTS FOUR KILLS!

I turned to help Randy to his feet when Lisa burst from the Hummer. I pulled my arms up to protect myself from another smack-down, but instead she drew her Sig P320 and screamed, "Down." Will and Stone appeared behind her with ARs shouldered in the same direction Lisa was aiming. A flash of panic tore through my head as I thought *She turned my own brother against me… he's going to help her kill me.* A millisecond later, Lisa took her first shot. I could hear the wasp-like buzz just over my head as I went to my knees with Randy in tow. Stone and Will followed Lisa's lead, bringing their weapons online. Duck-crawling behind the impromptu firing line, we got to our feet and searched for the instigation behind the team's action.

"What the f—" Randy was cut off by the intensifying assault.

Dozens of UCs blocked our route. UCs that appeared from nowhere. "Move, we need to protect our left flank," I said to Randy.

We snaked around the rear of the Hummer, coming to a stop across from the firing line. Lisa had advanced to a forward center position as Will and Stone wreaked havoc on the UCs on our right flank. With fewer UCs roaming our area, Randy and I targeted the fringes where the field grass met the shoulder guarding against another surprise attack.

"Did we just get ambushed?" Randy asked.

Before I could answer, Lisa let lose an angry yelp.

I followed the racket and found Lisa face down on the pavement. Her legs pumped wildly as she tried to kick free of the UC she had become entangled with. Lisa wasn't the easy meal the UC thought she was. It had her pinned to the pavement, but not immobilized, making it impossible to take a quick bite. She wasn't able to flip herself to face her assailant which would have allowed her to use a weapon to counter the attack. She pushed herself up, arching her back, and locked eyes with me. Something in them told me she was going to lose. On the move an instant later, screaming, "Fight, Lisa, keep fighting." I launched myself into the air as the UC moved in for a bite.

Chapter 21
Heavy Machines

"What's happening? Someone turn that damn alarm off," the senator yelled into the radio. He waited a full sixty-count and yelled again, "I SAID, what's happening? I also said turn the DAMN ALARM OFF. And I'm adding that you turn the lights back on." Still no response. He geared up for another scream when the guard poked his head through the door.

"Senator," he said, "LT asked that you shelter in place until we determine the threat level."

Emergency lighting illuminated the senator from above, giving him the appearance of a poorly aged goblin. The sight caused the guard to throw a shiver.

Disdain dripping from his stare, the senator asked, "What, pray-tell, is an LT?"

The question caught the young man off guard, and he figured it futile to answer the arrogant prick glued to his leather chair. Instead he said, "And the LT also said that you need to press the *big button* on the *talkie thing* if you want to reach him direct."

Without warning, the senator heaved a glass globe paperweight at the guard, heavy enough to crack his skull. The guard quickly slammed the door, causing the projectile to punch a hole in it at about head height. Behind the safety of the closed door, the guard yelled, "Oh, one more thing. You may want to try turning the *talkie thing* on. Makes a world of difference." His smirk morphed to a wide smile as the senator screeched, "SON OF A BITCH" accompanied by the sound of radio squelch.

The senator, now with a functioning radio, pressed the talk button and said, "Williams, what's happening? Why don't we have lights and why isn't the alarm shut off?"

After a ten-count, the radio squelched to life. Williams' voice boiled out, "The main generator ran out of fuel. We're running on emergency solar power, over."

In his patented arrogant tone, the senator said, "Well, Soldier-boy, fill the damn tank and get the lights back on."

After another ten-count, Williams replied, "You need to say *over* when speaking on a radio or I won't know if you finished your statement, over."

"When I'm no longer talking, that means I'm done. Now, why no lights? Fill the damn tank!"

"Well, Senator, I'd love to *fill the tank*. If we had diesel, you'd have lights, over."

"How is it you allowed us to run out of fuel, Williams? How did that happen?"

"Senator," Williams started. "Do you recall the conversation about wasting resources? I'm sure somewhere in that arrogant brain of yours you do. Well, this is what happens. We used all of our diesel filling the tugs. Tugs that never returned to port. Tugs that were being used to sate your lust for power."

Williams pulled away from the radio and barked orders to his men. Returning to the conversation, he added, "The loss of power disengaged the e-locks on the gate. Now dozens of the dead are shambling towards your building. I'd love to stop them, but I'm busy looking for fuel for the generator." Williams shut his radio off. He needed to prepare his men for the battle to come.

"If it has enough fuel, pull the dozer to the gate. We have to stop the flow!" Williams yelled at the seven men that had reported to duty when the alarm sounded. Of the seven, only three brought their BSU-issued guns. His total force numbered at thirty-six but only seven answered the call to duty. Only three carried guns. His assessment of the camp was grim; they were out of fuel, low on food and water, and now they might be eaten alive. All caused by political incompetence. *Today may be the day I rip the senator apart.* First, he had to stop the insurgence of zombies into the camp.

The seven men remained flatfooted after Williams gave the order to move the bulldozer. "What's wrong?" he asked, voice heavy with frustration. "Can any of you operate the dozer?"

To his surprise, two men raised a hand indicating they knew how to operate the machine. The understanding of what was happening shot his blood pressure through the top of his head. "Look, if you plan on surviving you must learn to take action independent of specific directions. Waiting for someone to tell you exactly what to do will get you, and every soul in this camp, killed."

With his frustration boiling over, he grabbed one of the two men by the front of his poorly fitted uniform and shoved him toward the hulking machine. "Start the machine. Drive the machine to the gate. Get as close as possible, then place the blade in front of the opening. DO NOT damage the gate. Is that clear enough, son?"

The young man, now resembling a scolded puppy, gave a curt nod and climbed to the cab of the dozer. He quickly familiarized himself with the controls, reached for the key and engaged the ignition. The behemoth bucked twice then belched black smoke as it roared to life. "She's running on fumes, sir. Fuel gage is pegged on empty."

Williams, restraining his impulse to crawl into the cab and throat-punch Captain Obvious, yelled over the clatter of the giant diesel motor, "Then move your ass." Eyes bugging at the LT's harsh delivery, the young man eased the dozer into gear and marched it towards the gate.

Williams turned to join his men in battle but was shocked to find his *force* planted in the same position as before. Not one had entered the fray. Civilians had taken up the fight using anything they could lay their hands on. Life and death struggles raged all around them, yet they stood perfectly still, looking to him for direction. With no time to dress them down, he capitulated to their need to have their hands held. He barked out orders in rapid secession, "You three, with the rifles, move to the gate. Do not shoot living people. Shoot any dead trying to get past the dozer. GO, NOW."

The men ran at the gate, weapons raised. To his horror, fingers were already on their triggers.

He watched as they ran out of sight then waited until he heard the first shot ring out. Other shots followed, bringing him some relief that they hadn't shot each other… yet.

He looked at the others. "Jesus H.… what's happening? We are losing our camp and you idiots haven't moved. GO. FIGHT. NOW."

A soldier whose name-tape identified him as Markesan, said, "Sir, with what? What do we use to fight?"

Williams broke. He couldn't believe it. Not only did they not bring their rifles, they brought not a single fighting instrument. Not even a rock.

Markesan was on the ground before Williams realized he had punched the young man. "Find a stick, a rock, a piece of broken glass and start defending your home. Watch me." When he finished screaming, he turned and ran to the closest monster. With skin waving in the air like a flag catching a lazy breeze, the monster let out a slimy-rasp as Williams approached. How they could see with the film covering their eyes baffled Williams, yet they locked onto their victims like heat-seeking missiles. This one must have been amazed that its food was delivering itself. Williams was three feet away when he went airborne, his right leg leading his flight. His calculations were perfect as his foot connected with the monster's nose. He felt crunching bone and cartilage as gravity and momentum slammed him to the ground with his foot remaining on the monster's distorted face. The sensation of facial bones collapsing was strangely satisfying. He wanted more.

He glanced at his troops as he searched for his next target. Although they had moved since he last checked, it was only to check on Markesan's condition. The soldier was up on one elbow, blood dribbling from his mouth and forming a puddle on the dirt in front of him.

Still enraged by the inaction of this group of idiots, Williams pointed and screamed, "If you are not fighting something by the time I reach your position, I will kill you myself."

Scattering like a slapstick skit, the group dispersed, except for Markesan. With his best mean-mug on display, the young soldier stared defiantly at Williams.

"When I reach you, I'm going to hobble you then feed you to the zombies. That should distract them long enough to allow me to kill more of them." He started in Markesan's direction, matching the young man's glare. In a singsong voice, he said "You're going to die."

Something in Williams' eyes convinced Markesan that he wasn't bluffing. He grabbed the handle of the small dagger hidden in his MOLLE vest and readied himself for Williams' arrival.

Markesan launched from the ground, dagger leading his attack. The shock in Williams' eyes filled the young soldier with confidence a moment before his world went dark.

Chapter 22
Cleveland Weather

The Black Hawk sat on the tarmac awaiting clearance, its burden heavy with eager war fighters hell-bent on retribution against the forces that had polluted their country with the dead. Each man was brimming with the weapons of war and each possessed the knowledge to employ them with malice.

The pilot, using open coms, said, "Sergeant Willis, we are still awaiting clearance. A cold front is moving through the region kicking up storms, some severe, to include hail."

Willis, no stranger to travel via Black Hawk said, "Warrant Officer Brooks, I've traveled in far worse, and in your copters. What's the deal? Also, I'm still just Willis to you and you're still a pain in the ass to me."

"Willis, you just made my day; it's good to know I live in your head enough to be a pain," Brooks replied.

With a slight chuckle, Willis said, "Well, Mr. Brooks, I have a big-ole brain with plenty of room for the less fortunate. So, what's the real reason we're delayed? Remember what I said about my brain. Don't BS me, good sir."

Covering his boom-mic, Brooks signaled Willis to come closer. Joining his friend near the cockpit, Willis asked, "What's up with the double secret communication?"

Brooks, face obscured by his masked helmet, said, "Other than the beautiful Cleveland weather, a VIP is arriving today. I'm not sure which blowhard it is. Nonetheless, Air Command orders are to target and destroy anything in the air at the same time as the VIP's bird. So, with that said, we will be *double secret vigilant* in getting our clearance."

Frustration on full display, Willis said, "Of course that's what it is. Because politicians still fancy themselves *the most important people alive*. Apparently, they're still in denial that they're the reason the virus even exists."

Willis turned to face his men and started to share the INTEL when Albright's voice broke over the radio. "Brooks, mission has been scrapped. I say again, your mission is scrapped. All flights are grounded. Willis, report to security room four immediately. Out."

Albright, always direct and military-proper, was more curt than normal. Something, or someone, had crawled under his skin. The breach at the Indiana and Illinois border was coming under control, but still eating resources. The issue at Entry Point One was fluid, but the latest sit-rep indicated they had contained it. Camp Hopkins had identified the source of the swelling UC population and would neutralize it in due time. It left Willis to question the reason for Albright's demeanor.

He arrived at security room four and entered after a quick knock. Albright, standing in front of a large wall-mounted map, greeted him with a brisk nod and said, "Willis, we have a change in plans for you and your men. We have decided to recon the BSU camp at Port Buffalo with drones prior to any assault. RAM-Brass has given the directive to limit civilian casualties. We are no longer planning a scorched earth campaign."

Willis bristled at the news. The civilians had aided and abetted the infiltration of UC into RAM, contributing to the deaths of hundreds of RAM citizens. This had the making of something more complex, something resembling a full military response to the threat not limited to their region.

With a solid read on Willis' thoughts, Albright said, "We don't have any further information, Willis. We're to stand down until RAM-Brass gives the order to move. And, if my instincts are correct, when we move on BSU, it'll be full-scale retaliation."

Willis said, "And, if my instincts are correct, that's not the only reason you called me here, sir. What else is happening?"

Albright moved to his desk and leaned on it with open palms. He looked at Willis and cut to the point, "Willis, MST1 ran into a cluster in Terra Alta. Hazelton sent them out with bad INTEL and no emergency extraction plan." After a long, uncomfortable, pause Albright said, "They lost two refugees and experienced a team casualty."

Willis squeezed his eyes shut and braced for the name of the fallen team member. "Jax Cunningham sacrificed his life for his team and country."

Willis felt a sense of relief. He hadn't conducted all of the training for MST1. He only knew of Jax through the status reports from Lewis and Stevenson. Randy and Otto were his key contacts. He'd made the mistake of befriending those two idiots; it would have shattered him if either was K.I.A.

His relief was fleeting as he recalled how highly the team thought of Jax. He was the guy you most wanted on your side: selfless, brave, and competent in his actions.

Albright hadn't finished delivering bad news and said, "MST2 has gone quiet. We dispatched them to Camp Whiting on the Indiana and Illinois border. Just south of Entry Point Four."

Willis allowed his frustration to control his mouth, and said, "Sir, what the hell are we doing?"

Albright gave Willis a puzzled stare.

Willis continued before his brain could shut him down. "With all due respect, sir, this is not how we sold the program to the MST. They should only police their own, well-defined, regions. We sent MST1 to West Virginia from Cleveland. Then sent MST2 to Indiana from Lansing. We didn't train them for the heavy engagements they faced in those areas. We assigned them sub-par vehicles and basic infantry weapons."

Willis gauged Albright's level of aggravation with him. When Albright didn't cut in, he continued, "We've sent them to be slaughtered, sir. We didn't train them for the intensity at the entry points. They're all fighters at heart and can survive small numbers of UCs, hell, even large numbers of them. But not the concentrations we see at the entry points. It's got to stop."

Albright waited a beat then responded, "Sergeant, the big picture dictated it. Has it occurred to you that a Chief Warrant Officer is running the day to day at Camp Hopkins? We are stretched that thin, Willis. Billings, our CO, is a First LT; the command structure for the region is headed by Major Ogle, not a colonel, but a major. We have hundreds of thousands of troops at the entry points. Tens of thousands more patrolling the border wall while running search and rescue missions. Thousands guarding hospitals and water treatment plants. The list goes on. Our Navy is bogged down evacuating our overseas assets and their families. They've set up blockades to defend against the inevitable hostile intrusion. Our Air Force is running hundreds of sorties behind BSU borders trying to slow the march of the UC. They're reporting devastation the likes we haven't seen since Hiroshima and Nagasaki."

Albright paused for effect and said, "Point being, we needed to push the envelope. We need RAM citizens to step ALL the way to the line and defend the homeland."

Willis understood what Albright was saying, and he didn't disagree that all of RAM would need to step up. But he broke from that thinking when it came to sending them into the meat grinders they'd been sent to. It was reckless. More importantly, they'd lied to the civilians that made up the MSTs.

"Sir, we told them they would ease the burden of the search and rescue functions. We told them it was to allow us to focus on the nuclear grid, to focus on the entry points, and the wall. We did not tell them they were going into full combat with the UC and with whoever is shooting at us from the BSU side of the wall."

The urge to walk out of the security center became overwhelming. Willis was a man of his word, and his military had just made him a liar. He was not okay with that. He understood that, by proxy, he had killed men and women, the men and women RAM needed now more than ever.

Albright, sensing Willis' irritation, said, "Do you want to talk to the people from the communities that supported the MST program? It may help you work through some of the emotions you're experiencing. We also need to tell them that we will intensify the program."

"I do, sir," Willis said.

"Dismissed," Albright said with a nod.

The battle in his mind consumed Willis as he walked the halls of the now fully militarized airport. He couldn't rationalize what he had been told. He wouldn't play a part of sacrificing another

RAM citizen. The MST expansion couldn't move forward, not the way Albright had described it!

Willis paused and gazed through the glass at the runway beyond, noticing the weather that had held up their mission had never arrived. *Well played, Albright.*

As he worked through a plan to stop the expansion of the MST program, two F22 Raptors roared from the sky and landed seconds apart. A risky maneuver Willis had never witnessed. As he watched them taxi from the runway, a large matte-black Boeing passenger jet landed. Two additional Raptors followed the plane until it touched down, then pulled off, remaining airborne and circling the airport. As soon as the Boeing cleared the runway, two F35 Lightning IIs appeared, seemingly from thin air, and landed. The two airborne Raptors made an additional pass over Hopkins then roared off in the direction they had come from. It was an impressive display of how to squander resources.

Politicians… still wasting time and money, he thought as he turned and headed to join his men.

Chapter 23
30-06

I traveled through the air like a guided missile seeking its rotted target. I braced for impact with the UC. I was so close now that I could smell the putrid stink radiating from its decomposing body. Imagine my surprise when it vanished. I panicked, thinking it had dropped out of sight as it took a chunk from Lisa's leg. An instant later, I landed squarely on Lisa's back. The *whooshing* sound escaping her lungs let me know I had successfully pushed all the air from Lisa's body. Well, at least the UC wasn't eating her. Relief and confusion blitzed my thoughts as I tried to locate the UC. What I found was Randy's big ole eyes staring back at me.

"Nice hang-time, Spidey," he said while pushing his knife through the UC's head. He had moved to aid Lisa the same instant I did and, apparently, had beaten me to it. He pulled the knife out with a hollow *thwack*, wiping the blade on the UC's shirt while searching for another target.

"Get off of me, you lummox," Lisa groaned. I ignored the Spiderman dig and the insult from Lisa long enough to get to my feet and help Lisa get to hers. Ready for another blast to my face from Lisa, I started to back away. Lisa, as expressive as ever, said, "Relax, Nancy-boy, I don't hate you anymore," following up with a begrudged, "thanks."

Through my now extremely swollen left eye, I may have caught a smile on her face.

Stone interrupted the bizarre moment. "Little help would be nice."

The battle persisted as Stone and Will held the line off our right flank. Lisa and Randy joined the fray while I took our left flank to ensure we didn't have another surprise guest.

"Did we get ambushed?" Will yelled over the din of battle, sending a spike through my gut.

Randy, between shots, said, "It seems like it, right? Like they laid in wait for us and launched an attack as a team." He continued, "Are they taking cover? Why do they keep dropping out of sight?"

The statement grabbed my attention, and I turned to witness the actions of the UC. The team had thinned the herd enough for us to make a tactical retreat.

"Load up, I'll take the wheel," I said. I turned to start my retreat, coming nose to mouth with a UC. My unique angle afforded me an unobstructed view of its badly damaged mouth. Torn lips and meat-littered teeth were less than two inches from the tip of my nose and closing fast. Shock stunted my reaction, only allowing me to pull my head back and away from the stinking maw. I brought my hands up, attempting to create distance when the monster's head disappeared in a bloody mist. I mean to say, it actually disappeared. The fine mist settled on my face as I stood stunned and unmoving.

Stone was the first to reach me and asked, "How'd you to do that?"

"I assumed one of you saved my ass. If not you, who? Or, maybe I caused it using my mind, because that's what I wished would happen."

We were gawking at the headless UC crumpled at our feet when a grizzled voice said, "Or maybe I saved your ass." After a five-count, it continued, "Did you actually believe you did it with your mind?" Followed by some snickering that made me feel right at home.

After the team killed the last of the UCs attacking from our right flank, they joined us. Again the disembodied voice traveled to us from a small area of undergrowth to our left. Randy fell back and readied his AR in a *just in case* move that would allow us a fighting chance if the voice morphed into a violent human.

I ignored the voice's question, mostly because I really thought I may have caused the UC's head to explode. (Stop it, we live in a world where dead people eat us. Does a little telekinesis sound so impossible?)

"I'd like to thank you in person. Can you show yourself? I'd like to shake your hand." I also wanted to flush the voice from cover to ensure we had a clear line of sight on him. You can't be too careful; until we achieved the guarantee of mutually assured destruction, I didn't trust him.

The undergrowth rustled as the man stood, his M1 Garand held at low ready. "Name's Max, Max Divination. Yes, that's my real name."

The man was about sixty-five and stood straight as an arrow; he was dressed in what I would describe as working-man clothes. Blue shirt and pants both smeared in grease with worn knees and elbows. I asked if I could approach him and he nodded. As I walked towards him, I couldn't help but admire the man's firearm. M1 Garands are superior rifles which served our military through several conflicts. It was chambered in thirty-aught-six, so it no longer surprised me that the UC's head had vanished.

You don't see them often, and its condition told me the gun was well-cared for.

As I halved the short distance, Max got a better look at me. He said, "Can you stop, please." And followed up with, "Son, what's your name?"

I said, "Otto, Otto Hammer. Yes, that's my real name."

A slight smile peeled back the right side of his mouth and he seemed to relax. "Well, Otto, you look like death. More importantly, you look infected. So, I'll take your word for it that you're happy I saved you. A person can't be too careful these days." He remained still a moment longer and said, "I'm going home. Be safe wherever your travels take you."

Max turned to walk away when Randy spoke up, "Max, I hate to ask more of you considering what you've already done for us. But, do you know where we can secure some diesel? We have a three-hour trip back to Cleveland and didn't refuel when we had the chance."

The news caught me by surprise, and I turned to face Randy with a questioning gaze.

"What? I wasn't the one driving when we left Hazelton, *Otto*. Was I? Nope, wasn't me. Who might that have been in the driver's seat, let's see? Oh, I remember, it was you, Otto."

"Wow, *Randy*, that was callous. I was surprised. I wasn't accusing you of anything. God, man, if you're still wondering why I forgot your last name, well, wonder no more," I shot back at him.

While I geared up for round two, Max broke in, "I hate to interrupt your discussion, but I may be able to help. What do you have for trade?" And there it was, the thing that would bring us back from the edge: RAM citizens working together. Capitalism at its finest. My chest swelled with pride and hope.

It hit me like a brick: HOPE. I stood in the middle of the road, bruised, battered, and covered in blood. Every part of my fifty-something-year-old body hurt and begged me to quit. We had lost so much over these weeks: friends, a secure future, and our way of life. But this one simple act felt like a first step towards reclaiming our world.

"Max," I started, "I'm sure we can make this work."

Max gave a quick nod and then put his thumb and pointer finger in his mouth and gave a sharp whistle. He said, "Let's head home. We have business to attend to."

It stunned me when four forms materialized from the tall field grass. As they came into focus, so too did their weapons. All were armed with AR platform long guns and several side arms. In the waning sunlight, it was easy to see all bore a strong resemblance to Max, both in features and dress. The action showed us we could trust Max. If he held ill intent, we would already be dead. And I'm sure he sensed the same of us.

"Follow the road for another hundred yards and turn west on the first dirt road you come to. That's my driveway; it's easy to miss, so keep your speed down." He glanced to his left and said, "Sidney, Mel, head to the gate. Don't open it until you can verify Otto and his friends are the people arriving. And check to make sure Otto hasn't changed." Two young men turned, without question, and headed northwest. He glanced to his right and said, "Mac, Ben, follow me. Otto, we'll see you in a few. Pull to the south side of the red outbuilding and wait till we come get you."

I nodded and the five of them melted away into the tall grass. The team joined me and we all clambered aboard our vehicle.

"What's the plan?" Will asked from the backseat.

I answered, "We have two thousand rounds of 5.56, two hundred rounds of .308, this crap military issue radio, one M4, and some other military issued goodies. Randy, what's the fuel situation?"

"Just under a quarter tank. We need roughly eighteen gallons to top off."

"Got it. We'll start at a thousand rounds of 5.56 and fifty rounds of .308 and a flash-bang. Get any food, weapons, or other items you're willing to part with ready. We need the fuel and trying to find it in a hostile environment while dodging the military is problematic. Let's do our best to close this deal." I was in my element. I could contribute to the team's success without causing physical damage to any of them.

We turned onto the heavily wooded dirt drive a minute later. "Let me do the negotiating. Keep your items in the Hummer until we need them. Make sure all of your magazines are full, so we have enough ammo for the trip home. Keep your side arms holstered but chamber a round now." I looked around the cab, meeting each set of eyes. "If this goes sideways, we go full-blown carpet-bombing on them. We clear on that?" Heads nodded while jaws set as we approached the gate.

We pulled to a stop at the gate and waited. The two young men were nowhere to be seen, but the raised hair on my arms told me we weren't alone.

Randy said, "One of them is to our right, in the undergrowth of that big oak. I haven't put eyes on his partner."

I said, "My Spidey-senses are telling me someone has crosshairs on my forehead. I'd have done the same. Probably waiting for me to change." Randy ignored my dig… I wasn't over it.

After a full two minutes, the oak tree guy moved to the gate, unlocked the enormous padlock and removed the chain. He waved us through as he pulled the single-hinged gate open. We followed the drive until we came to a clearing. I was impressed. Max didn't have a homestead, he had a compound. An impressive one at that. The grounds were free of clutter or garbage. A simple two-story house loomed to the north, resting on the edge of a circular drive. To the south sat three large outbuildings, each a different color, and again well- maintained. Several people tended one of the three massive garden-plots that flanked the outbuildings to the south. Young children ran in and out of the blue and white buildings engrossed in an intense game of hide-n-seek. Their squeals and laughter filled the air as they played, seemingly oblivious to the apocalypse.

Trees and thick brush bordered the entire property. A glint drew my eye to the barbed-wire strung in three levels inside the tree-line. If someone tried to enter from outside the property they wouldn't see it until it wrapped them up. It was genius-level strategy. Max had taken pride in his property well before and long after the virus spread. It sent my mind into overdrive trying to figure out what someone as well-positioned as Max might need from us. This may well be a tough negotiation.

The red outbuilding, standing half the size of a football field, was positioned furthest from the house. It was the only building lacking human activity. We pulled to the south as directed and found Max waiting for us. He stood with Mac and Ben to either side and motioned us to exit the Hummer. I opened my door and inquired about our weapons.

Max said, "You can carry them, leave them, whatever you're comfortable with. You'd be foolish to try something and I think you're smart enough to know that."

I looked around the cab and said, "We stick with the plan; leave the ARs in the Hummer."

Max grabbed the handle on the outbuilding's door, glanced back at me, and said, "Cleveland, you said you're from Cleveland, right?"

I nodded. "Yep."

Max said, "I thought that's what you said," and yanked the door open.

"What the!"

Chapter 24
Work For It

Markesan came to staring into a monster's visage centimeters from his own face. The taste of death was thick in his mouth as black drool fell from the zombie's open maw and entered Markesan's screaming mouth. His stomach roiled at the intrusion of the drool and heaved its meager contents into the monster's face. The splash back blinded him as it set off another round of retching. "What's happening? Help, somebody please HELP ME," he managed between his stomach's contractions. The sensation of his clothes being torn from his body pushed him to action. He tried to bring his left, then his right arm up to push the monster from his sight, but nothing happened. The realization that his limbs were restrained rocketed through him as he attempted to use his legs to shuffle away. Blades of pain cut his mind in half as the skin covering his abdomen split open.

The only part of his body he could move was his head. He used it to smash the face of the drooling nightmare hovering over him. The action allowed him a brief glance down his body. Thick rope, spiked to the ground, held his limbs and waist tight. Zombies pulled him apart and feasted on his flesh. More of them arrived as his screams pierced the air. Before they took his sight, he saw Williams to his left readying another spike. The man tilted his head and yelled, "You didn't want it bad enough. You didn't work for it." The realization that death had found him entered his mind as his skin left his body.

Williams gave the command to attack. The fear of being the next person spiked to the ground overrode the shock of the monsters feasting on Markesan. Soldiers and civilians descended on the undulating mass of dead as they gorged themselves. Clubs, knives, garden tools, and baseball bats laid waste to the dead. The wet sound of bone and brain splintering rose to a deafening pitch. Williams whipped the mob into a frenzy as he circled the group, ensuring all were doing their fair share of the killing.

"This is your home; you must defend it. These things came to rob you of your life, to eat your families, to end humanity." After pausing to kill one of the few corpses that didn't find a seat at the Markesan buffet, he continued his *inspirational* monologue. "Markesan didn't want to work for his safety, choosing to attack me instead of fighting for you and your families."

Bloodlust overtaking him, he found another dead straggler and shoved the spike though its left eye and through the back of its head. "Let this be a lesson to you. If you do not fight, you will not live. Your death will be excruciating. Your children will watch as you're eaten alive. FIGHT, FIGHT FOR YOUR LIVES."

Williams held vigilance over the onslaught until the last of the dead joined the heap of stinking carcasses piled high around Markesan's skeletal remains. He hoped this signaled a turning point for the survivors. That beginning today, they would take control of their lives and push back from the brink of extinction. Williams' hopes were dashed as he watched in disbelief as the triumphant mob just walked away from the mound of wasted humanity. Not one of them began to clear the bodies from the camp, as if accepting living with this mess was just part of life.

His ire turned to fury when he saw the young solider still sitting in the bulldozer's cab. "YOU," Williams started, "did you move at all?"

The young soldier feigned ignorance, pointed at himself as if saying *who, me?*

"What's your name, son?"

"Olson, James Olson, sir."

"Well, Olson, because of your heroic efforts I have reassigned you." Williams was dumbfounded when Olson smiled. *This dumbass thinks I'm complimenting him.* "You're now our environmental control manager." The smile on Olson's face grew as to threaten to tear his lips. He was receiving praise, and it made him ridiculously happy. Williams continued, "I'm happy to see you're happy. So, your new position requires you to… you're going to love this, Olson. It requires you to CLEAN THIS SHIT UP. Gather your squad mates, put on gloves, dig a big hole, place the bodies in the hole, burn the bodies. Have I been clear enough for you, Olson?"

Olson sat still in the cab, eyes wide and unblinking.

"NOW, Mr. Olson, move now. Or do you want to be next?" Williams barked.

Olson understood what Williams meant and literally launched himself from the bulldozer. He landed on legs already pumping to ensure his escape.

Williams called after him, "Oh, Mr. Olson, one more thing. Let the other men know I have two hundred yards of rope and thirty spikes."

Olson became a blur of arms and legs as he headed for the troop dorm.

Williams felt a perverse sense of amusement at the young man's distress. He would have started feeding his men to the undead weeks ago had he known it would have motivated them to action.

His fear of being left vulnerable to attack by sending his best troops into RAM had been realized. He grabbed his radio and turned it on. "Williams for Bantam, come in, over."

Nothing but static.

"Williams to Bantam, come in, over."

A burst of squelch preceded Bantam's response. "Go for Bantam."

Relieved to hear his only real soldier reply, he asked, "Is his royal majesty, Shafter, safe and accounted for, over?"

"Safe, accounted for, and locked in his office. I may have heard crying during the attack. Should I check on him? Over."

Williams chuckled and said, "Let the little man know I'm coming to visit him. And Bantam, start getting your things together. We may need a new home when I'm done. Out."

Bantam relished the thought of escaping Port Buffalo. "Roger that sir, out."

Williams grabbed a handful of spikes and headed to visit the senator.

Bantam slammed his fist on the locked door. The startled yelp from Shafter confirmed the level of fear the senator was living in.

"Senator, LT will join you soon."

Shafter began babbling something about respect and fear and his place in the world order.

Bantam yelled, "Senator, if you keep yelling you will attract the dead."

The silence from the office brought an evil grin to Bantam's face.

Chapter 25
Living Space

Pat was on her way to meet Darline at the quarantine area. They had set time aside to work with Dillan on upgraded security, and she was eager to get started. She arrived as Darline was explaining the community guidelines on quarantine to a highly agitated young lady.

"You'll be out in seventy-two hours, Nat. After that we move you into a new home."

Biting the inside of her cheek, Natalia said, "Can't they just move us into the new house and lock the door? We haven't been bitten or scratched or even have a paper cut."

"You must be quarantined for seventy-two hours. We make no exceptions. Nat, I need to get back to work, please ju—"

Pat cut in, "Young lady, my name is Pat Schreiber. This is our home. You will follow our rules while you live in our home. Grab your bags and report to quarantine." Pat stopped next to Darline and continued, "If you need any supplies you can request them after you're settled. Questions?"

Jack turned without uttering a word and started towards the assigned house. Natalia said, "Pat Schreiber, I'm Natalia Hammer. You're a scary person."

Pat nodded and said, "Pleased to meet you." She placed a hand on Darline's shoulder and said, "Dillan is waiting for us at my house; we should go."

Darline wrapped Natalia in her arms and told her she would stop later to check on her.

Dillan was sitting on Pat's porch when they arrived. He said, "I believe I've devised a strategy to stop the living and dead thirty feet from the fence."

Pat sensed the stress Dillan was feeling. She said, "You know this isn't your fault, right? No way could you, or any of us, have known they'd attack us like this. Someone strapped a bomb to a dead person, Dillan. You didn't open the gate for them."

Dillan said, "Pat, I know what you're doing, and I appreciate it, I do. The fact is I'm in charge of security. It's my job. No, it's my duty to keep this community safe." He locked eyes with Darline and said, "Your husband risked his life for me, Darline. Randy risked his life for me. Right now, they're risking their lives for this entire country. They deserve a safe place to sleep. We all deserve a safe place to sleep at night."

Darline recognized the commitment Dillan had to their security. It drove him to seek perfection. In that instant he transformed from the kid down the street to the man keeping them safe.

In her commanding style, Pat asked, "What's your plan? You said we need a thirty-foot buffer. Why?"

A grin grabbed Dillan's mouth. He pulled out several neatly folded pieces of paper and placed them on a small table. The pages held rough sketches depicting the community from an aerial view. The notes and symbols scribbled at various intervals on the map piqued Darline and Pat's interest.

Dillan started, "Darline, I'll need you to talk with Nila. I understand Randy may possess a bang-maker I can use for the perimeter." Receiving blanks stares he continued, "A little birdie told me Randy *may* own C4. I can use it along a tripwire. Think of it as the first line of defense."

Pat's eyes narrowed. "Dillan, we're not using C4 that close to the community. Actually, we're not using it at all. And why in God's name does Randy own C4?"

Forehead in hand, Darline said, "He doesn't. He thinks he does, but it's not real. Nila found it and used her company's resources to test it; they found no explosive compounds. The bricks are just clay. He bought them on the Internet, not even the dark web, just a weapons blog on the regular ole Internet. Nila should probably tell him before he gets himself killed trying to use it."

Dillan's body deflated, taking his soul with it. He'd hinged the first line of defense on that tripwire.

"Dillan, Otto has about a dozen perimeter alarms; probably more. The kind that use a 205-primer. I'm sure you can modify them to make a bigger bang. Would that work?"

As if born again, Dillan stood and grabbed Darline bear-hug-style and said, "I've always liked you. Ever since I was a kid, you've taken care of me."

Darline thought the reaction was a little strong, but it had been an emotional day and she felt it too.

Dillan detailed his plan to them. It was solid, a lot of work, but solid. With the focus now on stopping both UCs and fellow humans, they would build a second fence twenty feet out from the current fence. It would produce a much-needed buffer zone while creating better choke points, more time to react to threats, and more land for farming. Ten feet further out from the second fence they would install an early warning system consisting of simple metal wires strung at ankle and head height. Cans, bottles, and Otto's perimeter alarms would be attached to the wires. If anyone or anything tripped one, it would notify the guards of movement and elicit the appropriate response.

They had already cleared most of the surrounding houses of UCs and any useful supplies they held. Dozens of living residents had moved to their community. Many more people appeared to have retreated to either a military safe zone or other fallback position. This meant the plan shouldn't meet any short-term resistance. If residents returned to their scavenged homes or homes being merged into the community, it could get sticky. Dillan's teams started leaving notes inside the homes detailing what they'd removed and where to go for more information. It seemed the right thing to do.

"Well, get a move on, Dillan," Pat said. "Get with Joe Stevens about fencing. You'll need to pull together a construction crew..." She stopped herself. He knew what to do. "I'm sorry. Old habits. Get moving."

Dillan corralled his notes and headed down her driveway. He moved with haste; it was time to build.

Pat said, "Darline, when did I wake up in crazy town? Why in the world would your husband require exploding perimeter *thingies?* The better question, why would Randy need C4? What exactly did they have planned, a takeover of the *system?*"

Darline, unfazed by Pat's inference, said, "It kept him out of my hair, Pat. I drank a little wine, caught up on my reading, or did some shopping. He tinkered around getting us ready for the downfall of humanity. The trade worked for me and seemed harmless enough. Now, it appears they were way out-front of this mess."

Pat couldn't argue that last point. Had Otto not killed Beck and her boyfriend Kevin along with the Johnson twins that first night, their community could have been overrun.

Darline and Pat walked the streets together. The damage didn't seem as severe now that the chaos had ended. The homes that had sustained damage sported boarded-up windows and doors. *They should have already boarded their windows,* Darline concluded. *We were just shown the fence is not a failsafe. Individuals need to ensure the safety of life and property.*

"Seven people are injured," Pat started. "Two are critical. One, Bill Jenkins, might not survive. Over twenty-eight of them breached the fence but didn't even get thirty feet into our community. Our response was impressive but needs improvement. We need to initiate heavy training for all of us. And as much as I hate to admit it, we need Dillan's early engagement system."

The weight of responsibility on Pat's shoulders was obvious. Darline could see the wheels turning in her friend's mind. Pat continued, "We have much to maintain with limited resources. Our water supply worries me most. The pressure dropped over the last couple of days. Rob and his crew are tinkering with multistage pressure pumps. Although if the water is cut off, it won't matter. He keeps reminding me he and his crew are electricians, not city engineers. They built a makeshift electrical grid cobbled together with generators and alternative power supplies. But we don't know if it'll function or supply enough power for the entire community. Fuel becomes an issue if solar and wind is insufficient." Pat's eyes searched the horizon for answers but only found more questions. "We need food, water, and security. Darline, we need a plan by day's end."

Darline waited a beat to let Pat complete any unfinished thoughts. "Security first, Pat. Without security, the other things don't matter."

Pat showed a rare flash of vulnerability as she said, "Why would someone do this to us?"

Unable to answer, Darline simply took her friend's hand as they walked.

The old world was gone.

Chapter 26
Coward

The shrill voice belonging to Congresswomen Piles sent a quiver down Shafter's spine. "Piles, send an evacuation team NOW. We have no fuel, our food supply is near depleted, and I haven't showered in two days because of water rationing. We dumped seventy shipments in Cleveland. Mission completed!"

Piles, as usual, slurred and stuttered her response, "What has come of our arrangement with Mr. Kim? We should have our vaccine by now."

Shafter pulled the sat-phone from his ear. The question enraged him. This had been her plan from the start; now she was acting as if it fell solely on him. "I recall telling you to avoid this arrangement; I recall telling you not to trust him. As well, I recall that you told me to *suck it up*. Piles, you killed hundreds of millions of people y—"

Piles cut him short and said, "Correction, my dear, *we* killed hundreds of millions of people. And you are the only one stupid enough to allow yourself to be recorded negotiating with Kim. Rest assured we will pull through and we will bring RAM to its knees."

Shafter wiped sweat from his face. He would need to deal with her, to silence her. "Just send the evacuation team. We'll discuss this face to face."

After twenty seconds of incoherent babbling, Piles said, "We can only send resources for one person." The following pause may have been meant to elicit some honorable response about his wife. Or perhaps a solemn proclamation that he wouldn't leave a single person behind.

Instead he said, "I was only asking for one person."

Piles finished cackling and said, "You really are a saint. I expected you'd fail and arranged your exit weeks ago. Your evacuation team is already en route. ETA of forty-five minutes. Wait for them by the lighthouse. Move now and you'll be in Leamington by nightfall."

Shafter responded, "How will they land a helicopter... wait, Canada?"

Venom dripping from her words, Piles said, "You'll be traveling by boat. We lost our air force weeks ago. RAM caused our military to fracture; we barely have the resources to hold any of our assets. RAM made it so we had to relocate to foreign lands. They will pay, and your nasty little friend will help us exact our revenge and take our rightful place as leaders of the free world. Understand, we need Mr. Kim for more than the vaccine, and you'll make that happen."

The line went dead, and Shafter knew he had precious little time to escape. He frantically stuffed his briefcase with anything he could grab and started for the entrance to his private quarters. A forceful pounding on the office door startled him and he cried out in shock. The message delivered from the other side of the door set his pulse to racing. Trying to avoid raising suspicion, he spouted incoherent threats at the door and continued his retreat.

He walked into his quarters and found his wife passed out drunk on a threadbare sofa. The smell of vomit assaulting his senses, Shafter looked at his wife of thirty years and said, "My dear Agatha, I'll leave you the way I found you: drunk and alone." With not so much as a pang of guilt, he walked to the exit and, with caution, poked his head into the dying light. The pathway looked clear. The tennis courts to his right were void of the usual children at play. *Thank God for the breach*, he thought. If not, the courts would be infested with hundreds of tiny screeching hellions.

Water surrounded the Coast Guard Station on three sides, allowing them to forego fencing or other barriers needed to hold the dead at bay. He praised his own superior intellect for choosing the location. A short run to the parking lot then to the pathway leading to the lighthouse and he'd be safe. The sounds of chaos had died down and he knew Williams would soon discover his empty office. He estimated he had roughly thirty minutes until they discovered he wasn't hiding within the walls of the Sector Building. Agatha being present should cause them to think he had found a safe hiding place to wait out the attack. *No good man would leave his wife behind*. What fools they were. It would be far too late when they realized Agatha had been a marriage of political convenience. With wealthy parents and no ambition, she was the perfect fill-in for the role of dedicated wife. His smile surprised him, followed by the realization that he was happy to be done with her. He giggled like a child as he reached the path to the lighthouse.

Briefcase clutched to his chest, he cursed himself for insisting on wearing a suit every day. Sweat poured down his face as his Cole Haans slapped the unyielding pavement. He began searching for a place to hide his slender, spongy body until his rescue team arrived.

Shafter slipped on the slick pavement and tumbled down the stone-lined access to the break wall, causing him to lose his grip on the briefcase and nearly plummet into Lake Erie. Papers whipped around his head as he lay there catching his breath. As he got to his knees, he watched the contents of his briefcase blow across the stones and into the lake. "NO, this cannot happen," he cried. The BSU reunification plan had just vanished. With no secure laptop, he had recorded it by hand and now it was destroyed. Shafter scrambled to close the briefcase, salvaging what he could. Nearing a nervous breakdown, he reached into his pocket for the sat-phone but found only lint in his jacket pocket. He got to his feet a moment later, frantically patting each pocket repeatedly. The phone was missing. He searched the area around his fall but found nothing in the quickly vanishing sunlight.

The memory struck him like a baseball bat. The phone sat on his desk, exactly where he'd set it after his call with Piles. In his rush to exit, he'd forgotten the single most valuable tool he possessed: his connection to the DPRK. Without it he was useless to the Coalition. It represented the only power he wielded with them. *Wait, I'll relieve Piles of hers,* he thought as the tension left his body. *I still have Kim's direct line. He'll know the unrecognized number belongs to someone important. If not, the caller wouldn't have Dear Leader's number. It'll work, it has to work.* He pulled the briefcase back to his pigeon chest whilst completing his escape to the water's edge.

Wood exploded in every direction when Williams put his foot to the door. Spikes in hand, he barreled into Shafter's office. "Mr. Senator, I need to talk to you."

Williams found the office empty. He noticed the partially open door to Shafter's private quarters and began singing while he approached it, "Mr. Senator, it's not nice to hide from company." He slammed the door open to find Mrs. Shafter rising from the sofa, an empty bottle of Boones Farm held over her head, her only defensive choice.

She slurred something to the effect of, "My husband, the honorable senator, will have your a—." Her sentence cut off as she bent to expel the contents of her stomach. Williams judged from the stench this wasn't the first batch of cheap wine to liberate itself from her anorexic frame. She soon landed back on the sofa, unable to finish her tirade. Her head lost its battle with gravity as she passed out. Williams considered asking where her *honorable* husband had scurried off to, then realized she had returned to her usual condition: passed out drunk. She would have no idea of the location of the hole her little rat-bastard had tucked himself into.

Instead, Williams searched the four rooms of the small living quarters. The area resembled a ransacked house from a crime drama when he'd finished. Shafter hadn't exited through the office door, of that he was sure, leaving only one option. Williams bolted for the exterior exit. He took in the landscape, asking himself, "Where would I hide if I was a tiny, soft rat-bastard?"

The first outbuilding in the area seemed the logical choice, and that's why he ran towards the lighthouse. He was dealing with a politician; logic played no part in their decision-making process.

His knuckles white around the spikes, he ran at full speed to the one spot he knew he'd find the senator. Less than one hundred yards from his target, he heard the engine rumbling at idle. He pushed his body to its limit as the reality of what was happening sank in. At less than twenty yards, the powerful engine throttled up and the small brightly colored speedboat fled from the shore. Williams drew his sidearm, firing until the slide on his Para 1911 locked back.

The senator ducked behind the boat's bow and raised his hand, waving goodbye to Williams.

Shafter, unable to control his laughter, remained hidden long after he finished bidding farewell to Williams, his wife, but most of all the substandard living quarters. He was confident Piles would have secured a property matching their station in life.

He opened his briefcase to inventory what he had salvaged from his fall. But the first order of business was to kiss the piece of paper holding Mr. Kim's satellite phone number. He reached into the briefcase compartment that held the number, removing a folded yellow fragment of legal paper. He unfolded it and gasped. The paper held Piles' number. Frantic, he searched again and again. Tears ran down his cheeks as he turned the paper over to find a simple note:

Will always love you. XO Aggy.

His mind's eye showed him the location of what he searched for. It sat under the satellite phone, on his now abandoned desk.

Chapter 27
Top Off

The sight that greeted my eyes was awe-inspiring. I asked, "Max, whatcha got here?" Not in a hurry to answer my question, Max continued walking into the building. Following him, I told the team to hang back with Mac and Ben.

He said, "Otto, right?"

I nodded.

"Otto, this building holds the hard work of my family and friends. We started working on it after the very first reports came in from Times Square. Some of them were driven here by their owners, some we found. All of them now belong to us."

The full scope hit me as I followed Max deeper into the building. The building housed four fuel transport trailers complete with their semi-tractors. They sat nose to tail along the back of the building. To the front of the building were three smaller fuel carriers, similar to what airports used when fueling jets. Still large by most standards but not compared to the full-sized semis. The smaller trucks had "Kerosene" painted on them accompanied by a company logo for Divination Fuel Transport. Well, that answered my questions on how they'd ended up in Max Divination's building. He was the owner, with access to thousands of gallons of fuel, putting him in a powerful position in the coming months.

"How much fuel do you need? What do you have to trade, Otto?"

I'd gotten distracted looking around the building. It held much more than trucks and fuel. It appeared to be a workshop or mechanics garage. All manner of tools, lifting equipment, and containers were maintained in the same well-thought-out and uncluttered order as the rest of the property.

"Sorry, I was admiring your setup. I'm impressed, Max." He appeared uncomfortable with my comment, and I sensed a shift in his demeanor. Trying to get us back on track and put him at ease, I said, "Max, I really want to get home. I need nineteen gallons of diesel. I have four hundred rounds of 5.56 and twenty rounds of 308 I can part with."

Max, unmoved by my opening offer, appeared to do some math only he could see. When he finished, he said, "The going rate for twenty rounds of 5.56 in the old world was eight, maybe nine bucks. Diesel was going for about two dollars eighty cents a gallon, or about a third the cost of a box of twenty rounds of 5.56. Your offer comes in slightly over that ratio. Problem is, ammo is everywhere, fuel isn't. That inflates the cost of fuel to probably twenty dollars a gallon. Meaning you'll need to double your offer, Otto."

I blew my cheeks out in an *I can't afford that* expression while looking around the room. "Max, how about six hundred fifty for eighteen instead of nineteen gallons and I'll keep the .308 in the deal? Oh, and I can toss in a crap-ass military networking radio."

Max set a hard gaze on me and said, "Why would a group of soldiers try to trade a radio they know damn-well won't work in this area? Actually, Otto, that's offensive. I'm going to as—."

I interrupted him. "Max, two things. First, we are not actual military. The military asked us to assist them with searching for survivors. Second, did you say our radio won't work in this area?"

Confused by my response, Max explained further. Rightfully so, he thought we were military because of the Hummer and our appearance. The information about the radio was far more interesting. He told me that their walkie-talkies and other radios had been intermittently jammed. The whole area had the same issue. Red filled my vision while he told me of the issues he'd been having communicating with surrounding homesteads. What that meant was Hazelton was potentially aware, or might even be causing, radio interference and had never bothered to tell us. They simply sent us on our way, or more accurately sent us to our death.

Max asked, "You okay, Otto? You're making me a little nervous."

"Max, I'm good. I just had a revelation, and someone is going to answer some hard questions when I get home."

"Understood. I'll take your offer, but you can keep the radio." He stuck his hand out, and we shook on it.

He yelled for Mac to get things set up. As Mac approached, it became apparent that Mac was actually Maxine. She had also been jawing with Lisa. The net effect was plain to see. She already didn't like me, had never met me, never spoken to me, and might not even know my name. None of that mattered. Lisa had struck again.

While she glared at me, she asked Max, "They need diesel? Do you want them to fill up inside, or should I fill cans for them?"

Max gave the young lady a questioning look, and said, "Do it inside. If we're being watched, I don't want to show them that we're hiding fuel in here."

I said, "Max, let me get your ammo before you start."

He smiled and said, "Sure, but I would have donated it to you if I knew you weren't with the government. Don't trust them all that much, and they sure screwed-the-pooch this time. Although I suppose we need to push the world back to normal by doing normal things. So get the ammo, and we'll get you on the road home."

Max had a way about him. He was supremely confident with not a hint of arrogance. He had tight control over his homestead, and everyone seemed better for it. I had to set up a relationship between our communities. This man was a survivor.

After rejoining the group at the building's entrance, and following a lot of handshakes and thank yous, Randy asked no one in particular, "Did those UCs in the field ambush us? It sure seemed like it."

Ben cut in, "If you mean the way they appeared out of the grass, then no, they didn't. We've been encountering more UCs over the last five days. So we started setting up tripwire-spike traps coupled with patrols further away, trying to keep them at a safe distance. If they trip but miss the spike, they get up. It can be unsettling to watch them rise up like that. We had been tracking that group for about an hour when you arrived." He seemed irritated and paused a moment. "They're coming from the prison. You may have noticed the orange shirts and face tattoos. The prison guards set hundreds of them free as the infection spread. Should have killed them but instead let them loose for us to deal with."

Ben looked over at Mac and leaned in close to me, "I'm not sure what your friend said to Mac, but I'd steer clear of her if I were you."

I glanced at Lisa's smirking face and said, "I tried to save you. You remember that part, right?"

An exaggerated eye-roll later, she said, "Otto, please be quiet. Your voice is an assault on my ears."

"You, Lisa, are a mean person. A loud and mean person, so…"

She made a fake-out move at me, causing me to flinch. God, she was annoying!

"Max, do you have a spigot or well I can use to get some of this blood off my body?"

He was laughing at the exchange between me and Lisa.

"Otto, you have more problems than being covered in blood. You may want to keep an eye on this one." He dipped his head in Lisa's direction as he spoke. I detected Lisa gearing up for a rebuttal and swiftly cut her off.

"Max, I agree, but I really need some water splashed over my head. I'm a little smacked around if you haven't noticed. I think some cold water is in order."

Max led me to the well. Along the way we talked about what we'd witnessed at Entry Point One. I told him, in no uncertain terms, that if the Entry Point failed, his homestead would be overrun in a matter of hours.

"Max, the bombardment we were watching before the UC attack isn't a good sign. The slightest miscue, like an errant Howitzer round or downed copter hitting the gate or the wall, and it's over. The secondary gate surrounding the camp-proper was designed to keep people out, not tens-of-thousands of dead. How do we keep in touch with you?"

Max appeared to be viewing imaginary events unfold at some distant point. He turned and fixed me with a hard stare while he spoke, "Cell lines remain spotty and you know about the radios. We have a Ham Radio; it's been more reliable. Ben will give you our contact information. If your community doesn't have one, get one now. Contact us when you're set up. If the signal is good, we'll respond."

We arrived back at the building as Randy drove the Hummer from the cavernous red building, full of fuel and ready to carry us home. The sun had started its descent behind the trees on Max's property as we said our goodbyes. Mac and Lisa exchanged information while throwing their best stink-eyes my way. Yeah, I was looking forward to getting home.

As Randy wheeled north onto Route 20, he asked me, "Why'd you start the negotiation with such a lowball offer? We agreed to one thousand rounds."

"When I saw what Max had in his building, it changed things. He had more than I expected. We need the ammo more than he needs the fuel. Meaning he'd be more comfortable getting less because he feels secure in his position. That'll change in a few months." I watched the trees pass for a moment before continuing, "We need to go all-in on our security at home. And I'm talking all-in. What we witnessed at Entry Point One is a sign of things to come. The military will eventually run out of resources, and when they do the entry points will fail. We can only count on ourselves; we must become self-reliant. Big walls, big guns, producing our own food, water, and power. ALL-IN."

It had been about eleven hours since we'd started our ill-fated mission. In that short span we'd lost a friend, made new ones, saved and then lost two survivors, alienated an entire military base, and killed dozens of UCs. My aging body was starting to rebel from being pushed to its limit. Fighting the undead was turning into a young man's game and I questioned my role in the apocalypse. The deafening silence in the cab confirmed I wasn't alone in my questions about the path forward.

We were making good progress and would be home in less than three hours. A lot of meetings would be called in the coming days and weeks; the ones with the military would undoubtedly turn abrasive.

Stone hadn't uttered a word in over an hour; actually none of us had. Our mourning had begun. Our friend was gone, and I promised myself his death wouldn't be for naught. It would guide our path; of that I was confident.

Chapter 28
Their Own Voices

Williams sat at Shafter's desk riffling through drawers and files. It seemed the senator had left nothing useful behind. He grabbed a handful of files, intent on launching them skyward when he caught a glint in the dim emergency lighting. There it was, a satellite phone, still powered on.

"Why did you have a secret phone, Senator?" Williams asked no one. He grabbed the slender device and thumbed through the satellite phone's call history. The last call had happened during the attack. With no goal in mind, Williams chose the number and hit the call button. After several seconds, an unmistakable voice answered, "I'll talk to you when you arrive in Leamington. Your room is waiting. Now stop bothering me." The line went dead before Williams could speak.

"So, you're sliming your way to Canada. Good to know." Williams recorded the details that the woman had blurted out during the short, one-sided conversation. As he set the phone down, he noticed a yellow piece of paper. "Well, well, well what do we have here?" The paper held a series of numbers next to the inscription *KJU*.

Returning to the call history, he found a call to the number on the paper and hit send. After a much longer connection time, a heavily accented voice picked up. *"Why you call Dear Leader so early, Mr. Worm?"* Ice ran through Williams' veins. Why would Shafter call the DPRK?

His world closed in on him as the tumblers clicked into place. BSU had conspired with the DPRK to bring the virus to our shores.

"Put Mr. Kim on the line."

After a long pause, the voice said, "*I tell you before, Dear Leader no talk to worms. You sound funny. You sick or something? We can fix it, but we won't. We coming to stomp imperial scum, not help it. Dear Leader see you soon. He will crush you with mighty fists of rage.*"

No matter the country, politicians love the sound of their own voices, Williams mused when the line fell silent.

Shooting to his feet, he realized he had to find out who else Shafter was talking to. The bastard had sold out the world just to keep his power. Who else was responsible? Who else would Williams need to kill? *Where would a rat like Shafter hide phone numbers?* His eyes searched the room, landing on Shafter's chair; no, his throne. He grabbed the armrests and flipped Shafter's precious chair on its side. The hidden drawer became visible as the bottom of the chair was exposed. He kicked and slammed the chair until the drawer tore open and spit its contents to the floor.

Williams focused on a legal pad with two columns of writing. One was a series of numbers; the other appeared to be random letters. Williams recognized the letters for what they were, code. *Shafter wasn't the brightest*, he thought; this shouldn't be too difficult.

He studied the letters carefully and laughed. *You were so arrogant yet rudimentary. You deserve to die with your cohorts.* The senator had used a simple alphabet-mirror cipher, similar to what Williams used in third-grade to tell Fay Jones he liked her.

He picked the cipher at the top of the list with an asterisk on either side. It read: *WBVAG-PUVRS-ENZ*. Williams wrote the code key at the bottom of the page: A thru M with N thru Z directly below. Using the key, he spelled out: Joint Chief RAM. "Son of a... What were you chatting with RAM about?"

Williams stopped guessing and dialed the number. Two rings later, a voice displaying far too much calm in the face of world extinction filled the small speaker. "Shafter, have you come to your senses?"

Williams understood politicians, but military politicians played by different rules. They also possessed the means to eradicate a person from existence. If this was Chairman Mallet, he needed to navigate the conversation with extreme caution. He saw the path he needed to take; the only path that kept him alive. Hell, he might even save some people under his charge.

A voice rattling the speaker reached out and smacked him back to the moment. "Shafter, do not play with me. We are losing our world to monsters, we assume the DPRK will launch an offensive momentarily, and BSU hasn't confirmed the status of its nuclear power plants on our borders. I do NOT have time for games. Verbalize, NOW."

Williams said, "To whom am I speaking?" he thought the call had disconnected and began to ask again.

Then a voice so cold it froze him said, "You're speaking to the man who commands the power to eliminate you and your country from the planet. So, now that you possess that knowledge, I'll ask you. Who are you and where's Shafter?"

With nothing to lose, Williams figured he'd toss caution to the wind and said, "This is Lieutenant Williams, BSU Special Operations. Chairman Mallet, I think we can help each other."

Chapter 29
Home

The road home remained as clear as earlier in the day, with only the occasional UC showing a rotted head. I decided to record the streets and cities where I noticed communities being built. We The People would need to rebuild on our terms starting with establishing contact with others. It wouldn't be easy, but we could rebuild it. We could make it better than it was; better, stronger, and faster. A giggle escaped me as I quoted the opening monolog of the Six Million Dollar Man.

Without taking his eyes off the road, Randy said, "Care to share?"

My chuckle had been louder than I realized, and I wasn't planning to share the reason behind it. The ridicule would be unending and frankly, I'd taken enough abuse for one day.

Hoping to deflect, I said, "We should be within radio range of home. What are we, about an hour out?" My question created a stir. We needed to be home. And so far the ride felt like we had driven cross-country.

Will consulted our map and said, "At this pace, one hour until we're home. Forty minutes if we leave the military assigned route."

It was tempting, but we didn't know what waited for us off the predetermined route. I said, "I'd love to, but blundering into another hot mess isn't something I'm prepared for. We'll need to talk about that after we get settled back home."

Randy caught my veiled message and said, "What the hell does that mean? This team…"

I cut him off by grabbing the radio and snapping it on. "MST1 calling our community, do you copy?" I didn't realize I was holding my breath until Dillan replied. I exhaled for thirty seconds while he talked.

"Otto, we've been trying to raise you. We have news, but you first; tell me about the mission? Will the six of you be returning home in one piece?"

The question plowed into my emotions; I hadn't prepared for it. Unable to find my voice, my chin went to rest on my chest. I fought back the tears as I again attempted to speak.

Dillan came back hard, "OTTO, answer me. Tell me all six of you are coming home. We need to know that all six of you will sleep at home tonight."

I brought the radio to my mouth and forced out one word, "Jax." My voice shattered, and I released the talk button. Lisa placed a hand on my shoulder and reached for the radio from the backseat. I didn't object. This was all coming too fast, and I lost control of my emotions. I shoved my fingers against my tightly closed eyes, attempting to stem the flow. The action reminded me of the black and swollen eye I owned courtesy of Lisa. The sting pulled me from my emotional falter and refocused me on the most important lesson learned. We were responsible for our own safety; the military was up to its knees in shit. If one thing disturbed that shit-pile, we were all going to be covered in it.

Then Dillan told Lisa something that filled the cab with ice. Our community, our home, had been attacked. Moreover it was an organized attack utilizing the living and the dead. He told her we had seven people hurt, two critical.

Then he said, "Bill Jenkins may not make it. He took shrapnel to the chest. Durrell and Sabrina don't have the tools or training to go deep into someone's body. He also lost a lot of blood."

I'd heard enough. When Dillan finished, I held my hand up in a *pass the radio* gesture. I pressed the talk button and let loose a string of directions, "Dillan, we should be home in under an hour. We need to take a lot of action to secure our home. Let the community know a meeting will be held tomorrow. We need to fortify the gates and fences. We need to mobilize every resident to either produce or secure food, ammo, or weapons… no exceptions. See if you can procure any heavy construction equipment, like backhoes, bulldozers, and dump trucks. Something I saw at Camp Hazelton gave me an idea."

After pausing to breathe, I said, "You're a good man; your defenses saved our families, but we underestimated the situation. We are facing extinction, and brother, I'm not ready to disappear. Over."

"Got it. Also, your brother, Jackson, arrived during the attack. Sooo, your sister-in-law is a handful. She'll fit in nicely, over."

Stone slapped my arm and yelled, "HELL-YEAH!"

I pressed the talk button and said, "We needed that news, thanks. MST1 will be home soon. Otto, out."

Forty-eight minutes later we pulled up to the gate of our home. The overwhelming presence of armed citizens was reassuring. The condition of the fence was not. I said, "We have a ton of improvements to make. We'll get swallowed whole if even ten percent of the dead we saw at Entry Point One makes it to our home. Are you all ready to go medieval?"

Randy turned to me and said, "I've got the means to bring Hellfire down on ANYONE that rolls up on us."

A smile infringed on my somber mood; we would make this happen. We would fight!

We passed the bite inspection and exited the tents. But something very telling happened; we didn't just run to our loved ones crowded around the gate. We waited for each other to clear inspection. Then, shoulder to shoulder, we walked to the Hummer, got in and entered the community as a team.

Chapter 30
Acceptance

Captain Riggins manned the helm of his new tug. She was thirty years younger than the one resting on the bed of Lake Erie, with twice the power. The heavy chemical smell assaulted his senses, forcing him to hinge open all the windows protecting him from the elements. He risked another glance at the bloodstains covering the entire left side of the bridge, the bloodstains that used to be John. He tried to remove the remnants of his friend with every cleaning supply aboard the commandeered tug but only succeeded in creating a toxic mix of chemicals that threatened to render him unconscious.

The decision by Albright to allow them a choice of living in captivity or joining RAM in its fight for survival seemed an easy one. He would be free of confinement and on the water he loved. On top of that, this mission was focused on saving people, not flooding them with death, making it that much easier.

RAM needed to establish supply routes and utilizing the serpentine monster known as the Cuyahoga River was vital to this strategy. The steel mills, petroleum companies, and cement manufacturers lining the river's edge would play an essential role in fighting the dead. However, Riggins suspected the petroleum and oil were the most valuable of the commodities. It didn't matter to Riggins. He understood it like this: The more valuable the item, the more essential he became in delivering it to where it was needed.

Home was now the old cinderblock building that served as the dock master's offices in a former life. Their movement was restricted to the river and docks. One step past those barriers and life ended.

The offer came with very simple *advice*; if Riggins attempted to flee, he would be found and eliminated. "*We need you,*" Albright said, "*but we can make it without you. And I'm hoping you try because I'll be the one to kill you.*"

Riggins stared at the pistol sitting on the helm as he recalled Albright's words. The pistol he had used to kill his longtime friend, the man that was like a son to him.

"Why, John, why did you do it?" he thought aloud. "Tell me it didn't happen, please someone tell me he's still here." Anguish was thick in the words he spoke to the boat's empty bridge.

He relived the event as he navigated the twisting muddy river.

When Albright delivered them to the Port of Cleveland, John appeared ecstatic to be back on the water. They ran safety and supply checks, checked her for seaworthiness, and fired up the big beautiful diesel engines. All of her gauges sprang into action, signifying she had been well cared for.

The harbor master, a grizzled seadog going by the name Slips, directed him to take the tug on a quick run to the breakwall and back.

He pulled Riggins to the side and told him, "I've been told to end your life at the first sign of trouble. Understand; I'll do as I'm told, without hesitation."

About two hundred yards from the wall, John told the captain to keep going. Run her back to Port Buffalo, he said. "We're free, Captain. The fools set us free."

Riggins looked at his friend and shook his head, "John, they will kill us ten minutes outside the breakwall. You've seen what they're capable of. You need to accept this life. Resisting it will serve only to break your soul."

The betrayal in John's eyes blistered Riggins with guilt. It morphed into bright red hatred in a matter of seconds. "Are you joking? They'll kill us once they no longer need us. They killed some of our friends; they're going to kill every person living in Port Buffalo. We need to warn them; we need to get home and warn them."

Riggins pulled the throttle to full-stop and faced the young man. The tug drifted towards the breakwall as Riggins pleaded with his longtime friend. "John, get that fool notion out of your head. Our own government killed us long ago, not RAM. Those people we left behind care about no one but themselves and have already sealed their fate. They focused solely on taking over RAM. Never a word about what was being done to save BSU." Riggins turned back to the helm and steered the tug starboard, slowing the wall's approach. "We will stay. RAM is home now. Our thoughts of revenge need to end. Accept it, John."

With the engine at idle, the sound of a semi-auto slide being racked was unmistakable. Riggins' head instinctively shot in the direction of the deadly sound. The sight defied logic. John pointed an ancient-looking handgun at the captain's head. Instinct overrode loyalty as he moved at John with the agility of a man half his age. Before his mind regained control, John lay on the deck bleeding from a head wound. The Colt Model 1908 rested in the growing puddle of John's life force. The inscription on the gun's slide bore the same name as the tug: Tug Off.

That was three days ago. Each day since he'd questioned the walls of the bridge. *Why did Slip leave the gun behind?* But mostly he begged his friend to forgive him.

Chapter 31
Re-assigned

Willis sat quietly in a Humvee as his anger simmered. He watched as no less than twelve soldiers escorted the political trio to a sleek luxury motor coach. *This is a joke, right? We wouldn't waste our time with this; it makes no sense.*

He attempted to occupy his thoughts with something other than blowing the coach and its occupants sky high. Willis studied the luxury vehicle more closely. The flat black paint resembled the coatings used on the F117 Night Hawk. The wheel wells were enclosed by thick steel that extended to the middle of the tire. Not unusual on its own, except all four-wheel wells were covered, and the density of the steel was impressive. The bus appeared windowless save for the small pivoting gun ports placed every three feet.

As he continued his visual inspection, a six-foot section of the driver's side slowly hinged open. The slab of steel lowered, exposing the largest TV Willis had seen outside of a football stadium. At the same time, an array of antennas and satellite dishes raised from the roof joining three large shark-fin receivers atop the luxury motor coach. Willis and Stevenson looked at each other with eyebrows raised at the impressive display.

Stevenson asked, "Whatcha think, they trying to contact the Space Station with all of that?"

Willis nodded. "Looks like that's the goal. *To the moon, Alice.*"

Stevenson looked a question at Willis, to which Willis replied, "Jackie Gleason, you know him? He was probably on your grandparents' TV when you visited them for Thanksgiving. Funny old dude, always threatening to punch someone."

Stevenson, still blank faced, broke off the stare and said, "What the hell is that?"

Willis followed Stevenson's gaze and almost died from laughter. There, in vivid *Technicolor*, eight feet high by twelve feet wide, was the face of Vice President Pace.

After reality set in and the laughter stopped, Willis said, "Are you shitting me? We're going to escort these idiots while they go stumping on the campaign trail?" Memories of the apology tour his dad had complained about, before the Split, came to mind. A waste of time, effort, and assets.

The giant face of the VP began repeating the word *Testing*. After the fifteenth time, Willis reached the end of his tolerance. He sprang from the Humvee and moved to the bus like a streak of lightening. Stevenson heard him blurt something to the effect of, "I've got a test for you. I'm going to test my foot in your ass."

Two of the guards recognized Willis and gave a passive response to the well-respected leader of war-fighters. "Hey Sarge, this is a restricted area."

He fixed them with a hard stare and yelled, "Stand down, soldiers, I have a message for the talking heads."

With eyes on his advance, two hard-looking, well-armed men dressed in black ACUs approached Willis. They were calm in their demeanor, but moved with haste to intercept the agitated man.

"Sergeant, I believe the corporal advised you on the restricted area."

Willis studied the men. They appeared battle-tested and confident in their movements yet void of arrogance. Both were a muscular, clean-shaven, six-plus-feet with intense eyes and scar-covered knuckles. Willis knew that testing their training would be a mistake, and probably his last. Nonetheless, he had some wisdom to impart to the idiot on the TV.

The black ACUs held no identifying markings; Willis figured that before the virus, neither man had existed in government records. Willis chose his words with care and said, "Gentlemen, I'm Sergeant Willis out of Camp Hopkins. I've been tapped to assist with security; I'd like to meet the person I'm risking my life and the lives of my men for." When he spoke about his men, he shuddered at putting them in harm's way for blowhard politicians.

Understanding splashed across their features. The leader of the two men glanced over his shoulder and told his partner to return to his previous position guarding the door of the motor coach.

"Willis, your reputation precedes you. You and your men hit it hard at the onset of the virus. Helped stop the surge here, and in the communities surrounding the Camp. I was hoping I'd meet you. Albright tells me soldiers request to be under your leadership, and the ones that are, would gladly walk through fire for you."

In a show of respect, the man offered his hand to Willis, and the sergeant gripped it in a firm shake. The words and actions of the man knocked Willis off his game plan. His desire to place his boot in the VP's ass subsided, but only slightly.

"The man you asked to speak to also requested time with you. He was adamant that the meeting should only take place if it doesn't interfere with your duties. Let me clear the visit. I'll be back in ten."

Willis wasn't sure if he meant ten seconds or minutes but didn't ask. His mind was too busy asking *What's happening?* This wasn't how it unfolded when the idea sprang into his head. He figured he'd be locked in a cell by now, or worse.

The man appeared from the entrance and waved Willis over. Stevenson exited the Humvee, M4 in hand, and said, "Whoa, what's up, Sergeant?"

Willis said, "We're good, Stevenson. I'll be back in five." He followed with a wink and nod. Stevenson got the message and started the countdown.

"Stevenson's reaction is what I was talking about earlier," the man said to Willis as he entered the motor coach. "I've had more than one sergeant that I would have gladly delivered to the enemy. But not that one; he was ready to go full-balls on us to save you."

Willis didn't see the big deal; he would have done the same for Stevenson if roles were reversed. That's how his squad operated. Willis asked the man for his name, but he just smiled and told him to move to the main area of the motor coach.

The Vice President greeted Willis the instant he entered the cramped area. The VP was flanked by two familiar faces which Willis couldn't put names to. He was surprised to find all three politicians dressed in dark-earth tactical uniforms, each with a sidearm on their hip. A dozen men and women bustled around the tight confines. They monitored countless computer screens, radios, and other communication devices, some of which

Willis had never seen. The organized chaos was broken by the occasional spoken report of places confirmed as still living.

One young woman cracked her head on equipment overhanging her position in her exuberance to relay an update. It didn't stop her as she reported, "North and West Akron reporting living communities!" Her announcement was followed by high-fives and fist pumps.

"Sergeant Willis, I'm Vice President Pace. Soldier, I'm in your debt. My entire family is in your debt."

This was coming at Willis much too fast; he'd planned to be on the offensive, putting the smack-down on bloated politicians. Instead, he was impressed with the efforts of the men and women surrounding him.

Wait, what did the VP just say? "Excuse me, sir, but I'm not clear on your meaning?"

Pace stepped close and grabbed Willis by his shoulders.

Please don't try to kiss me, he thought. He braced for the awkward moment he'd conjured up in his head, but instead the VP said, "You saved my daughter."

Willis, thrown another curveball, grabbed his shoulder radio and said, "Stevenson, give me ten more." A knowing smile creased the hard-featured mug of the nameless man in black.

"Sir, I don't recall being on guard detail for a high-profile VIP such as your daughter. I believe you have me confused with another solider."

Pace released Willis from his grip and stepped back. "She wasn't under guard. We have a strained relationship, my daughter and I. She lives in New York. Manhattan, to be exact. She changed her name fifteen years ago and left home. Hell, she left our entire state." Pace seemed to flash through some painful memories before he continued. "She was in this very airport, in town on business, waiting on her flight home. Her trip cut short by news of the virus' rapid spread, she thought New York would be safer. Fewer people with guns. She told me how everyone at the gate knew something was wrong when the arriving plane approached the jet way. It almost crashed into the windows overlooking the tarmac. The screams of the passengers and crew filled the gate area as soon as the jet way door opened…"

Pace was interrupted buy another shout: "Living confirmed in the city of Parma." The announcement was followed by the same excited cheers as the Akron announcement.

The Vice President turned his attention back to Willis and pushed on with his story. "The living pushed, shoved, and crawled over each other trying to exit that plane. The panic motivated many in the gate area to forego their flight and head for the exits. My daughter, Debbie, hesitated before deciding to retreat. By the time she did, the dead had entered the gate area. She turned to run, but the monsters filling the concourse as they spilled from other gates cut her off. She took refuge in a diner and prepared to fight to her death. Armed with only a spatula, she started swinging at anything that moved."

"That was your daughter! I remember her; she was kicking some UC butt when we found her. She fell right in with us; not a stitch of hesitation as we corralled survivors to the EVAC point, unlike some other unlucky souls who stutter-stepped to their deaths." Willis didn't share how attractive he'd found her. Pace was her dad, and technically his boss, so he kept it to himself.

Pace broke a giant, pride-filled smile at the story Willis relayed. "She told me you and your men *cleared a path through the dead, like a Yankees outfielder on his way to the end- zone.* Debbie isn't a sports fan; she just knows I'm not a Yankees fan, so she uses them whenever she can to dig at me. The thing that impressed her most was the way you used abandoned cars to secure the pickup zone for their extraction... Anyway, I'm rambling on. I thank you; my family is whole because of your actions."

The interaction with Pace humbled Willis. His chest pumped with pride for his men. Even so, he still didn't know the goal of today's mission. "Sir, thank you. I work with some fine men, and it's good to hear that we made a difference. Speaking of my men, what is our mission today? Because, and with all due respect, if you're just campaigning, I'd rather not risk the lives of my men for something meaningless."

Pace locked eyes with Willis and said, "Sergeant, gather your men. I have a lot of information to share."

Willis and Stevenson stood quietly while digesting the news from the VP. Willis broke from his stupor and said, "Mr. Vice President, I need to get one of my men reassigned to my squad. He's been sent to work hospital security, but I need him with me. It might delay your tour, but I need him."

VP Pace, unfazed, said, "Willis, we have several hours before we can even think about talking to our survivors. Get your man, take care of your business, and we'll radio you when we need you."

As they exited the motor-coach, Willis said, "Stevenson, we're going to get Lewis. Then we need to visit Otto."

Chapter 32
Sleepy Man

I awoke to crinkling plastic, and Lisa cackling in some distant part of my home. The clock read 6 A.M., meaning I'd squeezed in less than seven hours of sleep before the bane of my existence ruined my morning.

The previous night was a blank spot in my mind, I remembered driving through the gate, exiting the Hummer, and falling into Darline's arms. I certainly couldn't recall why I was sleeping on a plastic-covered bed!

I decided that Lisa made me cranky and started to get out of bed to enlighten her with that knowledge. Then it hit me. I slept in the guest room, on plastic, fully clothed less my boots. Even during a zombie apocalypse Darline refused to let our sheets get sullied with the filth of battle that smeared the length of my body. Getting a whiff of myself, I decided I couldn't blame her for banishing me. I was a bit overripe.

When I stood, the trials of yesterday reminded me of my age. I stumbled from the shock-wave of pain and decided I needed to take a less direct path to a standing position. My sight was blurry, chiefly in my left eye. It seemed like it was covered in glue as my attempt to open it was met with far too much resistance. I reached up to touch it and was greeted with a jolt of pain. *Ooooh yes, now I remember.* Much like the pain of being in her presence, Lisa was the cause of my painful left eye.

At that moment, another gregarious chortle reached my ears. "Lisaaaa, are you trying to kill me?" I barked while attempting, once again, to stand, this time using the nightstand as leverage. A sound akin to grinding glass resonated from my knees accompanied by firecracker-like pops from my lower back. I went still, waiting for the pain to hit, but mercifully it never came. One baby step at a time, I trundled my way out of the room. I needed some dramatic flair to cover my little old man shuffle lest Lisa ridicule my condition. So I bellowed again, "Why are you in my house a mere seven hours after I finally got to sleep?" The house fell vacuum-chamber silent. Only the sound of my shuffling aging body broke the stillness.

I paused at the top of the stairs; I was a little intimidated by the thought of using them. It would be a long bumpy fall if I miss-navigated. A real possibility given my current physical condition. Suddenly, Darline's smiling face appeared from the doorway leading to the kitchen at the bottom of the staircase.

"Hello, sleepyhead. I'm happy you finally decided to join us."

I was so happy to see her face and hear her voice, I almost lost my edge. But I recognized what was happening. She'd deployed the classic maneuver developed by women hundreds of years ago and honed to a razor's edge. She had begun the *disarm and conquer maneuver*. The maneuver comprises one, or several, tactics designed to throw a man off his game. Make him forget why he's mad or interrupt a tirade of logic. They treat us like putty they're molding into a shape of their choosing.

Well, not today. I sucked a gulp of air and prepared my counterattack. But Darline said, "Do you need some help with the stairs?" She was so sincere it completely disarmed me. I nodded with the enthusiasm of a puppy and waited as she ascended the staircase and offered me a shoulder for support.

It almost worked; I had almost allowed her to *mold* me into docility. Then we crossed the threshold into the kitchen, and there she sat. The queen of destruction, the spawn of Hell, the mother of all things unholy. Lisa! A crooked, mocking grin joined evil raised eyebrows to form a face found only in documentaries about the criminally insane.

I needed to rebound, so I said, "Darline, your friend almost shot me AND she punched me… in the face, hard. We should remove her from our home, from our sanctuary." I made a rookie mistake with the sanctuary part.

"Well, Otto, what might have caused Lisa to punch you? Is it possible she simply reacted to an unpleasant comment or action?" Darline is a master at the *mold* maneuver. I needed to adapt and overcome if I wanted to land any punches. But I was so sleepy. I just wanted to turn on the TV and watch football, or baseball, hell I'd even watch golf if it meant life had returned to normal. (Okay, definitely not golf.)

Through the fog of this war, I said, "I have no idea what would have caused her to act like a fanatical and abusive person. I thought things were progressing nicely."

Lisa snorted and Darline removed her shoulder from my armpit. Clinging to hope I said, "Oh, so now you're taking her side? The side of an attempted murderer and sworn Otto hater." *Dramatic pause.* "I'm going to take a shower and visit Jack and Natalia in quarantine. It'll be nice to be amongst friends."

Darline shook her head and said, "Well, you better hurry, they get out of quarantine in fifteen minutes."

"What?" I said "How can that be? They got here yesterday. We can't let them out; family or not, they need to stay in quarantine."

Lisa cackled and said, "Oh, I can't wait to see this." I gave a sharp look to the demon spawn and turned back to Darline.

"See what, Darline? What does the *fiend* want to see?"

Darline took my grubby paws in hers and said, "Otto, you've been sleeping for nearly two days."

Well, that was shocking news. "That explains why I need to pee so bad. My bladder is about three times its normal size." I wasn't exaggerating. I really needed to go to the bathroom. It was just so far away that I considered asking for an empty plastic water bottle. Like she was reading my mind, Darline ordered me upstairs to relieve myself and wash away the filth and stink I'd accumulated over the last several days.

Lisa, ever the antagonist, yelled after me, "Be careful, Mister Van Winkle. We wouldn't want you to fall down, pee yourself, and fall back to sleep. Or, perhaps, considering your age, you should catch another two or three days of sleep."

With my back to the kitchen, and to Lisa, I climbed the stairs one painful step at a time. I said, "I'm not Dutch, and *twenty-two* for *twenty*... Wilma." I heard the legs of her chair scrape along the hardwood, like she was going to chase me. I believe, had she come after me, I would have shot her because I really wasn't in the mood to see her stupid face.

Chapter 33
The Brothers Hammer and Randy

Showered, shaved, and fed, I started to feel better. I limped, still had a black eye, my back worried me, and I wanted to go back to bed. So, marginally better.

I limped my way outside and found a big ole F250 sitting in the driveway. *It must be Christmas morning*! Darline had remembered to get me a new vehicle, like I'd asked after the Jeep died. I figured she was going to get me a scooter, or some other mean-spirited mode of transportation. But no, I laid eyes upon a full-sized man truck.

Poking her head out the front door, Darline said, "Hey, glad I caught you. Take your brother's truck to him for me, will you? We parked it here until they cleared quarantine." She tossed the keys in my direction; I ignored them as they fell to the ground. Darline screwed up her face and asked "What, moving too fast for you to catch?"

I glanced at the truck then to Darline and asked, "This isn't for me? It isn't the replacement for the Jeep?"

Darline didn't skip a beat. "You are kidding, right? At what point should I have scooted off to get your majesty a new truck? After the breach? Oh, I know, after we cleaned up the remnants of the attack? No wait, while I was checking on you every hour to make sure you were still breathing for the last two days?" The door slammed as she stomped into the house.

I have some really mean people in my life, I mused as I picked up the keys and climbed into the truck. I also made a *note to self* to get more details on the breach. However, I wanted to see my brothers, and I wanted to see them NOW.

By brothers I meant all of them, that included Randy, if, of course he was still talking to me. I never really knew with him, and the incident with his last name could prove an issue worthy of the silent treatment.

Nila answered the door with her welcoming smile. They weren't expecting me, but it never mattered with her. She always treated me like family.

Randy appeared at the door before I could properly greet his better half. His mean-mug signaled something wasn't right with his world.

"I'm leaving with Otto. We can finish talking later." Then he barreled through the door. No hug, no kiss, no goodbye. He just walked out, didn't even acknowledge me. He walked to the truck and got in the passenger side and stared straight ahead.

Nila said, "Someone got some upsetting news about one of his toys. It wasn't received well."

Perfect. My already long day just got a dose of miserable added to it. I lost two days to Van Winkle sleep, woke up to Lisa in my home, and now Randy was salty.

"Nila, do I even want to know what happened to set him off? Did something happen to one of his guns?"

Nila seemed to pity me for how Randy was about to behave. She shook her head and said, "Otto, I'm sorry. I'm sure Randy will tell you ALL about it." She peered over my shoulder, at her pouting husband, and asked, "How are you feeling? You've been out of commission for a long while. Everything okay?"

My face flashed hot with embarrassment, "I'm good, all good, nothing to see here."

Nila smiled, tilted her head, and said, "Well, your eye is telling a different story. I guess *Wilma* fought back." And there it was. The *mean wives club* strikes again.

Hooking a thumb at the truck, I said, "I'm just going to go. You know, Randy awaits, and we got stuff to do. So, bye." I scurried to the truck before I suffered any more embarrassment.

"Why are our wives so mean," I said as I put the truck in gear. Randy seemed to have a miniature psychotic-break. His eyes went wide as saucers and he screamed so loud I almost jumped from the truck cab from the shock.

"It's just clay, simple clay wrapped in C4 packaging, Otto. I can't believe it. You can't trust a single person. Not one single person. I hope the bastard that sold me CLAY is shuffling around waiting for a bullet to the forehead!"

That didn't take long! And he wasn't finished. "Nila knew, Otto, she knew about it, she discovered the sham and kept it to herself! She hid the truth from me for years, man. Just let me believe I had the best toy in the whole damn city!" He stifled a sob. Poor bastard. "I've been made a fool of, Otto. A damn fool! Someone needs to pay for this. Can we go on a run outside the gate? I need to go to Youngstown, hour-thirty to and an hour-thirty back. It's a quick trip!"

The reference to Youngstown answered my questions from weeks earlier about where he'd bought the C4. Had he told me Youngstown when I first asked, I wouldn't have questioned that it was legit C4 (The Sopranos weren't kidding).

"No, Randy, we cannot put the apocalypse on hold, travel to Youngstown, and search for a conman who may already be dead.

Or better yet, who may actually own real C4 and is waiting for you to show up."

Randy accepted my answer as I had expected, poorly. His response started with his patented crazy eye glare, graduated to flared nostrils moving air through them like a steam-pump, and finished with his mouth opening to level a counterattack. But I cut him off by telling him, "We are going to see Jack and Stone; we're having a meeting of the brothers. We need to create a solid security plan. We'll present it to Dillan, Pat, and the others after we button it up."

Randy started to talk over me, and then finally absorbed what I said. "Brothers, a meeting of the brothers? You mean Jack, Stone, you *and* me? Like we are all brothers and having a meeting, the *four* of us. Four brothers, getting some plans in place…"

I held up my hand. "Randy, you can say it as many ways as you'd like; it always ends with the same answer." Finally, peace and quiet from the passenger seat!

Randy was an only child, and it showed at times like this. He'd always wanted a brother, so this meant a lot to him. I also knew how to use his desire to my advantage, and I felt zero guilt for doing it.

We pulled into the driveway of Jack's new home in time to find him and Stone struggling to remove a couch from the house. The work was being performed under Natalia's watchful eye. She appeared to be doing a thorough job of *supervising while giving direction* to Jack and Stone.

Not a chance she'd be happy about me pulling my brothers away from the task; nevertheless, it had to be done. *Might as well have one more woman yelling at me,* I decided as I parked the truck.

Natalia didn't wait a millisecond before reacting to our arrival. "Otto, I'm thrilled that you're alive, but your brothers are busy. So, whatever shenanigans you're planning need to wait. Who's this?" she asked, nodding at Randy. "Another troublemaker come to distract my husband?" It sounded worse than it was; she gave me a hug after her sharp words.

"Good to see you, Nat. I couldn't be any happier that you two live here now. This troublemaker is Randy."

Finger wagging at Randy, she said, "No crap. Men at work. And nice to meet you."

Randy only managed to get a nod in before she turned away.

We walked towards the house, and Jack and Stone set the couch down. "Hey, I thought you slipped into a coma, you've been out for days," Stone said. "Must be that fifty-something-year-old body of yours."

My entire family is mean! I brushed the comment off and grabbed my brothers in a group hug. I pulled my head up and noticed Randy's sorrowful expression as he watched the three of us.

"Walk it in and hug it out, Randy." He was on us like a UC on fresh meat.

It was good to have this group together. I felt stronger for it. Stronger and better.

Chapter 34
Our Only Way Forward

Jack and Stone tried recruiting me and Randy to help move the couch to the garage. Feeling just north of crippled, I passed on the offer and helped Natalia supervise the move. When they finished, the four brothers started on a plan.

Jack started the meeting by displaying too much common sense. "I want to make sure I understand something. Dillan has been managing the community's security. He's kept everyone safe since day one, created security patrols, organized scavenging missions, and is at this very second executing his new plan for the fence. Are those true statements?" Not waiting for an answer, he continued. "And now, for whatever reason, you believe we can do a better job than him. So much better, in fact, we didn't ask him to join us. Or, should I say, Otto and Randy didn't ask Dillan when they decided to talk about our security. Do I understand that correctly? So, you're okay with undermining the guy who the entire community trusts with their lives?" Another brief pause. "A guy, from what I understand, is respected far more than Otto? So, Otto, are you clear on the ramifications of such an action?"

Jack paused. I waited long enough to ensure he wasn't baiting me into speaking just to cut me off with more common sense. I said, "Ouch, Jackson. That respect part was uncalled for. I'll be keeping your truck after the character assassination."

Jack grinned and said, "You don't know what character assassination means, do you?"

"Natalia, I want you to know that you can stay after we kick your husband out of the community." I'm not sure I was joking.

Jack brought it back to the point he was making, and it was a good point. "All I'm saying is that ANY conversation regarding security needs to involve Dillan. You may even find that after two days of sleep, he has already started or finished some of the things you've only been thinking about."

Not true, I thought, because none of my ideas were solidified. They were comprised of several hundred random ideas that when strung together may or may not form a plan. And I needed to organize them before we had our community meeting.

I grabbed my radio and hailed Dillan, telling him it was time to continue our talk. The one we'd started on the radio when MST1 returned from our mission. He was working the fence and sounded none-too-pleased to be pulled away. But he agreed to join us anyway.

Dillan arrived about ten minutes after I radioed him. Hot, sweaty, and exhausted, he cut to the point. "What do you want? Oh, by the way, it's also good to see you up and around. I put the community meeting on hold until you got back on your feet. Nice shiner. Looks like Lisa has a vicious right-cross."

I bristled at the comment, but knowing he and Lisa may be an item, I let it slide.

"Thanks for coming, Dillan. It's good to be awake. Every part of my body hurts, but it's still good to be awake. We want to talk about what we witnessed and what needs to be done to protect our community. Grab a seat, it'll take a while. You may also find yourself glad to have taken that seat after you hear the story."

Dillan joined us at the dining room table and, with furrowed brows, asked, "What's going on, Otto?"

I debated how to convey the information and decided on the direct approach. So, I leaned in and gave him both barrels, so to speak. I shared what we'd witnessed at Entry Point One, the amount of humanity attempting to enter RAM, and the amount of them being slaughtered by the dead. But the information that grabbed his short-hairs was the military bombardment of all moving things on BSU soil. It drove home the realization that the situation had spiraled. If the military can't hold the line, it was up to us to hold it. He went a pale-green color at the news. Actually, we all turned a shade of pale-green while revisiting that fateful moment.

"Dillan, we need to approach security differently. The fence needs to be updated and reinforced to repel thousands of UCs, not the hundreds it can hold back now. We need to prepare for attacks by the living and the dead. I gave it some thought, and I'd like your input."

Dillan pulled a small notepad from his back pocket then a pen from his shirt pocket. He glanced quickly at all the brothers, then locked on me, giving a stiff nod. Reading from his notes, he told us about the current plan to engage threats thirty feet from the main gate and informing me that Darline had volunteered my perimeter alarms. No new car and giving away my toys… she's a *nice* lady!

It was a solid plan for stopping hundreds of UC and slimy human combatants, that is. We could build on his plan. Make it work to repel larger numbers of walking death.

Dillan asked, "What do you think about moving out even further, possibly fifty or maybe seventy yards? We don't have the resources to build the type of wall RAM built at the border. But if we employ multiple barriers, like pit-traps with pikes, Jersey Barriers, and earth-walls between houses, we can thin their numbers before they reach our main fence. It gives us time to assess and react to the threat." Dillan had dedicated a lot of thought to our security. And I liked all of his ideas.

Then he offered something that gobsmacked us. "We have two small, lower-end drones. We found them in items left behind by people who migrated to the safe zones. I want to use them to provide long-range surveillance. Make it impossible for people to blindside us." He was ready, more ready than any of us, to start the transformation of our community to a self-reliant refuge for the living. He understood that it was our only way forward.

I was going to hug him, maybe kiss the brilliant SOB, but this was a very manly meeting, so I just told him that he was f-ing brilliant.

I told him I'd like to create crews to manufacture ammunition and pledged both my XL650 and DL-SBD loading presses. Randy pledged his Hornady, Lock-and-Load AP. And we both volunteered to train and assist with the machines. We talked about firearms training for every person in the community. The entire population needed to be confident enough to pull the trigger in anger when necessary. He floated the idea of organizing some teenagers into gun cleaning teams to keep our firearms functioning and expose them to the diverse collection of firearms the community possessed.

Unbeknownst to Will, we elected him leader of firearms training and hand-to-hand combat. Or, at a minimum, some defensive techniques.

We needed to secure a HAM radio, something none of us knew anything about. Jack jumped on the opportunity to join the conversation, but it wasn't productive. "Wait, none of you own a HAM? Your little prepper group never thought to pick up something for long-range or state-to-state communications?" The comment received three hard stares that served to quiet Jack, but didn't stop him from looking smug.

"Hey, Jack. Do you possess a HAM radio we can use? Or, how about any radio at all? Oh, wait, your tiny radio was left behind, with all of your other supplies when…"

Stone cut in, "Enough, you two. We're not thirteen fighting over the last piece of pizza. Get focused."

Never one to let arguments die easy or quick deaths, I said, "He started it, I was just finishing it."

My attention was brought back to the conversation by Dillan snapping his fingers in my face. "What, what… what do you want?" I barked.

"I want to get back to building a plan to save our lives. But if you and Jack fancy going fisticuffs, head outside, the grownups have work to do." He had a point, a snotty way of saying it, but a point nonetheless. I shot Jack one last mean-mug and refocused.

We decided that checking for HAM antennas on cars and homes while we scavenged would be phase one in finding a HAM. If in two weeks we didn't find one, we'd hit some big-box stores in search of one.

The search for heavy construction equipment wasn't going as hoped. The community's resident contractor only had access to two large dump trucks and the semi he used to transport the fencing. It was a start, but not enough.

Dillan said, "Jay is getting a group geared up to go after the trucks. We've been seeing an increasing number of UCs in the area, so we're loading the group up with enough firepower to punch through anything they encounter. The uptick in UC activity has been steady since we first noticed it just before you all started MST training. I can't shake the feeling it has something to do with the attack."

That news caused a stir in the group. Stone looked around the table and said, "Looks like we're heading outside the gate again. Let's wrap up and locate Jay. He'll need an escort."

Dillan grabbed his radio and hailed Jay and told him to delay his exit. Jay was psyched to hear about the extra guns joining him. He put his trip on ice and was waiting for us to meet up with him.

"All right then, we covered most of what we needed to. We'll revisit the details on the fence and who'll be overseeing the other initiatives, but we're heading in the right direction. So, let's roll." I tried to stand and froze in place. My red face, cheeks bulging with air, and pathetic groan tipped everyone, including me, to my poor physical condition. I wasn't able to stand as I pushed on the table trying to pivot myself upright.

It was no use; I couldn't get vertical. Seems like those low-back pops from when I got out of bed had finally revealed their true intention. Pain shot down both legs and radiated up my spine. My arms gave out, and I came down hard in my chair as my head hit the table, sending yet another wave of pain coursing around my old body. *This may be the most depressing moment of my life*, I thought as I opened my eyes and raised my head enough to see the stunned faces of the group.

Stone and Jack moved in my direction, but I called them off. If I moved at this moment, I would surely die. "Please, don't touch me," I said. "Do you have any pain meds? Anything? A handful of baby aspirin. I'll take anything. But please, for the love of God, don't touch me."

I sounded so pathetic even I pitied me. I sat, chest resting on the table, neck bent sideways, arms splayed and useless, while begging for some painkillers. Natalia, drawn to the ruckus, walked in and took charge.

"Oh, Jesus, what the hell happened to you? Is this because of Lisa punching you?"

I was in too much pain and just said, "Probably, she's a tough one. I'll say whatever you want to hear about Lisa if it'll get me a painkiller? Do you have Aleve or Ibuprofen, maybe a gun to put me out of my misery?"

Natalia moved like a rocket and started searching all the kitchen cabinets for something to help me. I told the team to head out. We couldn't stop because I'm old and crippled. Jack, with much trepidation, asked, "Um, are you guys looking for me to join you?"

Stone answered, "Well, Jack, with Otto out of commission and Dillan working the fence, yes we are. Ultimately, you're a member of this community now; you'll need to find a role that supports it. You may as well see how you fit into MST1. Grab your gun, get your boots laced up, and let's roll."

Jack moved with indecision looking for boots, his gun, and ammo. He ran to the kitchen and grabbed a steak knife and gave Natalia a kiss.

"Don't get yourself killed, please. You still have furniture to move," she told Jack as she searched cabinets and drawers.

"Thanks babe, I'll try my best."

She faced him and hugged him tight. "I said please, so you're obligated to come home safe."

"Hey, kids. I love the smooch-face, but I need some pain meds and the team needs to get moving. So, kiss, hug, and return to your assigned tasks. Thanks, love ya both." I was in so much pain that I started sweating and didn't have time for the lovey-dovey stuff. I had to get back on my feet, or at least get my face off the table and assume a normal seated position. Moreover, the community needed to get moving on its updated security plan. So they needed to wrap it up!

Jack walked past me and flicked my ear and told me to *get well soon* in that mocking voice he's used since we were kids. The one that often led to full blown fist-fights, which I typically lost. Maybe we should ask him to leave the community; I'm sure the military safe zones still have room.

While the team walked out the front door, I heard Stone ask, "Jack, did you bring a steak knife as a weapon? Don't answer, I know what I saw. When we get back, we're going to get you situated with some useful tools."

Jack, sounding hurt, could only muster a sad little response. "You know, I'm older than Otto, I'm the oldest of the three of us. If you all did that to Otto, what do you think will happen to me?"

Stone laughed and laughed and laughed at Jack. I wanted to join him, but it would have hurt.

I was going to ask Natalia to radio Darline when she slammed a bottle of Aleve and some water on the table. She had to force feed me the five Aleve I requested, but I managed to swallow them all. Now, I wait for relief to find me and pray I'm not permanently stuck in this position.

Chapter 35
How To Save Yourself

"Williams, I'm going to need a good-faith gesture before anyone is rescued from your safe zone. So, start talking."

Williams could tell that Chairman Mallet wasn't in a negotiating mood. He wanted answers, he wanted them now, and he wouldn't hesitate to bomb the safe zone to dust if he was pushed. Williams had requested EVAC assistance for the zone, but had never communicated the number of people to be saved. One thing was certain; he would be one of the evacuees.

"How many refugees is RAM willing to receive? We housed around two hundred, but after the breach, I'm not sure of the population."

Seconds ticked by in slow motion as he waited for Mallet to respond. When he did, Williams recognized his mistake immediately. "Williams, you've been breached? You may have infected people that you aren't aware of? Is that what you're telling me?"

Williams gripped the phone tight as he worked on a response that wouldn't get them all killed. Finally, he gave the only answer he could if he wanted to live. "Two, Chairman, you'll be picking up two survivors." He figured he was already going to Hell, so he may as well buy himself as much time on Earth as possible.

"We won't be picking up a single person until you give me information I can use."

Williams decided to give up enough to get the EVAC started. "BSU had two dozen teams operating in RAM. I say *had* because I haven't made contact with them in over a week. Their multipronged mission is to facilitate the downfall of any RAM civilian outposts, tie up RAM military resources, and secure land that BSU can launch additional missions from. Any of RAM's shoreline communities are in jeopardy."

He knew the information wasn't enough to save him, so he kept talking. "The locations of units under my command form a fan pattern beginning three miles due south of Edgewater Beach, Cleveland. Then, draw a straight line east to west and place a circle every six miles. Those are the locations of our troops, with our command center in the city of Cleveland at West 117th and Bellaire, occupying a Dollar Store. Approximate force size for all locations combined was seventy-five young, poorly trained men."

Williams' chest grew tight when he gave up the information on his men. He'd just signed their death warrants. He took solace in two things: he wouldn't have to inform their families they had been killed, and, if he put hands on Shafter, he would rip him into seventy-five individual pieces.

"Oh, I also know where Shafter holed up. That's all you get until me and my plus-one are safe on RAM soil."

"Be in the field next to the lighthouse in seven minutes. RAM Black Hawks are in the air. You arrive with more than your plus-one, RAM will sanitize all of you. Mallet, out."

Williams bolted to the door just as the senator's wife emerged from her quarters. "I'm your plus one, right? You're committed to keeping me safe and alive and I heard you say you

162

know where my husband is." Her hand trembled as it gripped a small overnight bag, probably filled with booze.

Williams pulled his Para 1911 and sent a .45 ACP hollow point slamming through her forehead. As a bloody mist settled on the walls, Williams said, "No one cares about you; I did you a favor."

Bantam blasted into the office, M4 ready. "Time to go, Bantam. You have three minutes to gather your essentials. We rally next to the lighthouse in four. Asses and elbows, son." Bantam's jaw hinged wide, but Williams spoke first. "I said asses and elbows… move out."

The sound of a copter thumping in the distance prompted them to action. "I've got what I need, Williams. I'm ready to EVAC."

With a curt nod, Williams led the way.

As they entered the field to the west of the lighthouse, a bright light appeared several miles offshore. It approached much faster than he expected. The reality hit Williams a millisecond before the Hellfire Missile blazed overhead. The camp was being sterilized. It was probably the plan even before he talked to Mallet. The copters arrived too quickly for it to be anything else. His phone call with Mallet had saved their lives!

The first Hellfire hit the main housing building, ripping into it with a brilliant display of power. Soon the sky was alight with bright exhaust plumes that trailed swarms of Hellfires. Explosions shook the ground as hysterical residents scrambled from flaming buildings.

Two AH-64 Apaches roared overhead and converged on the main gate. The fleeing residents piled atop the bulldozer blocking the breach as they attempted to escape through the malfunctioning gate. When they touched ground on the other side, death at the mouths of monsters greeted them.

The only mercy shown by the Apache pilots came as they brought their M230 Chain-guns to life. Both the living and dead exploded as the rounds found flesh. The screams of the living were silenced seconds after the hail of thirty-millimeter projectiles began raining from the sky.

Additional Apaches floated over the camp while laying waste to Williams' former home. The warbirds from the gate pulled off and began strafing the lake surrounding the camp as the living took to the water to escape the dual onslaught of military machines and dead mouths.

Engrossed in the destruction, Williams and Bantam were unaware of the Black Hawk approaching behind them. When a blinding light flooded the area, Williams knew it secured their survival. The Black Hawk's rotor wash vanquished the heat radiating from the flaming camp while drowning the screams of the dying as it descended to the field.

Williams grabbed Bantam by the shoulder and pulled him toward the open cabin door. The sudden appearance of the door gunner pointing the hot end of an M134 Gatling-gun in their direction forced a hard stop mere feet from the safety of the Black Hawk cabin.

The door gunner frantically signaled them to get down, and both men slammed themselves to the hard pack. Hands covering his helmetless head, Williams registered the unmistakable growl of two thousand rounds per minute exiting the M134. When the maelstrom ceased, they were instantly on the move.

After heaving into the Black Hawk, Williams twisted to see the gunner's target. The sight caused gooseflesh to cover his body. Dozens of broken bodies covered the ground less than fifteen feet from where they last stood. Unable to determine if the bodies were living or dead before their introduction to the projectiles spit from the M134, Williams rationalized that it just didn't matter. He lived, that's all that counted.

He looked at Bantam who was on his back gasping for air, when the vision disappeared and his hands were forced together, then restrained. The sack over his head was cinched tight just below his bottom jaw. The sharp edge of a knife at his throat ended his struggle.

"I'm Chief Warrant Officer Albright. I look forward to slitting your throat if needed."

He stopped his fight against the restraints. The force of the Black Hawk lifting off pushed him harder to the floor. He prayed Albright had control on the knife at his neck.

"I've been ordered to kill you both if my questions aren't answered. The same order holds true for less than truthful answers." Albright removed the knife and said, "Where is Shafter located?"

Williams gulped hard. "Got enough fuel to get to Canada?"

Chapter 36
Patricia's Wrath

Lewis may have been trying to speak, but Pat didn't care. She hadn't stopped talking since Lewis made the mistake of saying no to her and made the bigger mistake of telling her why. She gripped the radio with crushing force and said, "Lewis, I need to understand something. You won't EVAC two of our wounded until after the visit by some VIP whose name you can't tell me. Who couldn't care less about what we've been through? A person who will be guarded by resources this community only dreams of having. Is that what you're telling me?"

Lewis opened his mouth when Pat revived her verbal assault. "I'll tell you what, Lewis. We will bring them to you. I will drive them through the front damn doors of that hospital, directly to the check-in counter. Then, I'm going to find you. Do you know why? Because you sound like my son. And when my son acted like this, the only thing he'd listen to was my foot in his ass. Have I been clear, young man?"

To avoid being interrupted again, Lewis waited out the silence. He pressed the talk button and said, "Pat, resources are the problem. Yes, the VIP is eating them up. As are the UC shuffling the streets. They are—."

Pat spoke over him. "Are you being condescending? Are you fanning the flames with superciliousness?"

Lewis recovered only slightly, asking, "Pat, what does supercili-whatever, even mean? Don't answer. I'm sure I don't want to know. My hands are tied. I have no one to send for your wounded. I promise you, I would if I could. Look, I should be with my squad, but I'm running the show at a hospital. Do you think that makes me happy?"

Pat wasn't used to losing an argument, and she was determined not to lose this one. "Lewis, I'll be bringing them to you. And I'm bringing a vial of blood that we need tested. We've lost over a dozen people to the virus; we will not lose another. Not one more. Tell the hospital to prepare for our arrival. Tell your men to stand down when we arrive. Because I promise you, Lewis, we will fight back. Clear enough?"

Before Lewis could stop himself, he responded, "Yes Mom, I mean Ma'am."

Pat grinned; *the angry mom routine works again. Men are so simple.* "Very good, we'll advise you when we head out. Pat out."

Lewis sat back in his chair. He felt like his drill sergeant had given him a very public dressing-down. He looked over at the wide-eyed private seated next to him and said, "That woman is terrifying."

Chapter 37
Meeting Your Match

Pat's smug smile wasn't helping Lewis' mood, so he was thankful when Willis broke the tension. "I need to find Otto. Lewis, you and Stevenson secure the wounded. Pat, when you finish gloating, please arrange to have a vial of Andy's blood drawn. You'll find the needed supplies in the ambulance."

A question was burning up Lewis' brain. "Why not administer a test from the kits MST1 brought back?"

Pat went steely. "We did. The solution turned gray. Three times, three different kits, always gray."

Lewis wasn't sure what to make of Pat's revelation and simply ended the conversation. Speculating about the results would take them to dark places.

On the soldier's heels, Pat entered the makeshift hospital. Durrell greeted them and quickly led them to the converted first-floor bedroom housing the wounded. "Bill's condition worsens every hour; he's bleeding internally and needs surgery to remove the shrapnel." Durrell met Sabrina's eyes as he entered the room.

"Thank God you're taking him," she exclaimed. "We've reached our limit. Bill needs a hospital, ASAP. He needs blood transfusions. We lack the supplies to perform transfusions." Stuffing a manila folder in Lewis' hand, Sabrina said, "These are their charts; radio with questions. Just, please, get moving. He's slipping away."

Lewis stepped past Durrell and Sabrina and ordered Stevenson to retrieve a body-board from the military ambulance. He stood silent for a moment, taking in the situation. The urgency was real; these people needed a hospital. "Pat, time is not our friend. Get Andy ready. You'll need to do that now."

The military tone threw Pat. In the normal world, she would have railed against Lewis' direction. Instead, she smiled and said, "We already have it refrigerated. Durrell drew the sample after our *conversation*."

Lewis was impressed to find that Pat hadn't been bluffing. She'd planned to drive through the doors of the hospital just like she'd promised. Lewis regarded the tough seventy-something community matriarch and realized he had met his match.

Pat winked and marched to the kitchen to retrieve the sample. Stevenson passed by with the board and the relocation of the wounded began in earnest.

Relief swept over Pat as the soldiers secured the two wounded citizens to the bunk-style cots in the cavernous ambulance. "You're right; you have met your match. But I'm grateful for everything you've done."

Lewis raised his eyebrows. "How'd you know I was thinking that?"

Pat gave a warm smile and said, "I told you, you remind me of my son."

Lewis returned the smile. "You're still a scary woman. But you already know that."

Chapter 38
A Visitor

After a full thirty-four minutes, and five more Aleve, I managed to force myself upright. I was still stuck in the chair at the table, but I was upright. Baby steps!

Natalia busied herself putting a personal touch on her new home, leaving me to my own devices. Meaning, I pushed myself up inch by inch and then remained perfectly still, staring at the wall in the dining room.

While I admired a picture of the Cleveland skyline, Natalia removed it. Apparently, she didn't like it and wasn't concerned that it functioned as my singular distraction from the pain. It left me to replay the events from Terra Alta, which reignited my anger towards the military. After things settled in the community, Willis would get a big-fat-earful of my feelings about the MST program.

After fuming for ten minutes, the first urges to pee tugged at my bladder. I had no idea how I'd accomplish that task, but it wouldn't involve my sister-in-law. Wetting myself seemed a better option at this point.

Figuring she'd still be perturbed, I had avoided radioing Darline, but this development mandated her involvement.

I grabbed the radio, instantly regretting my quick movement. I remained still while the shards of glass inhabiting my back ceased their migration. The sound of a diesel engine entering the driveway pulled my attention to the window at the opposite end of the dining room. More shards of glass migrated as my head turned and I tried to identify the origin of the engine.

Our sole Hummer was currently in use by the team. I didn't recall any other diesels in the community, so this one was a mystery. I forced my hand to my holstered XDm, resting my palm on its grip. Surprises and mysteries were bad things lately, so I wanted to be ready to mount a defense if needed. A feeble defense, but a defense nonetheless. The thought of peeing myself in the middle of a fight flashed through my mind. So, if I didn't neutralize the threat as it entered the house, I'd be able to shoot it while it laughed at me. Win-win!

Natalia breezed through the room, cutting off the visitor's knock. "Come in, come in. I'm Natalia, and Mr. Otto is stuck at the table in the dining room."

Who the hell was she talking to, and how'd she know they were coming for me? I felt betrayed; my own family had conspired against me.

Then a familiar voice said, "Nice to meet you, ma'am. I'm Sergeant Willis. I'll only be a moment."

Things got quiet, with hushed voices exchanging information. The front door was blocked by the dining room entryway wall. But I pictured the dorky smile on the man-boy's face beaming bright at the news of my current condition.

"Stop gossiping about me, Willis, and get your ass in here. We need to talk."

The room went crickets-silent until Natalia said, "See, that's what I meant."

"Thanks, my favorite sister-in-law, appreciate the support. Thanksgiving should be fun this year because you're no longer invited." It was as lame a comeback as it sounds.

The young man with whom I was presently unhappy walked his big head into the dining room a moment later.

"If I could stand, I'd be boxing you about the head and shoulders. You are so low on my list of favorite people that you've crossed over to the list of people I don't like. You know Jax is dead, right? And the stupid MST program almost got us all killed, right?"

Willis didn't flinch at my words, and that kinda pissed me off. He needed to experience my anger; he needed to know where he stood with me. He was no better than the politicians he answered to. Just another government thug exploiting RAM citizens. Well, that ended when Jax sacrificed his life.

Willis hesitated, then opened his mouth to talk, but I cut him short. "I'm not done. Did I say I was done? I don't recall surrendering the floor to you. You'll know when I'm finished. Then, and only then, you can talk." I was talking in circles as anger clouded my thoughts, making it difficult to form a sentence. And, of course, that angered me even more!

"Why are you here, Willis? If you tell me it's to send the team out on another mission I will summon all of my strength to stand and when I do, you may want to exit the area." It was a bluff, of course. On my best day, I couldn't take Willis. He knew it, I knew it, everyone in the house knew it. But it sounded, and felt, good to say! With a bug-eyed nod, I surrendered the floor to him.

"Otto, I'm sorry about what happened. That wasn't how the MSTs were to be utilized, but desperate times called for it. I'm sure you remember what you witnessed at Entry Point One. Well, it gets worse. Entry Point Four is contained but just barely, and now we know why. Also, the Western Entry Points are under siege by millions of UCs... But before I continue, I have news."

Willis was out of character, fidgety and hurried. It was clear he wasn't supposed to be here and didn't have time for my temper tantrum. He told me that VP Pace would visit our community sometime today. The VP would give the community an update on our progress against the virus, our survivor counts, and go forward strategy as a nation.

He took an awkward pause in the middle of a sentence and it was clear he had much more information to share and was searching for a way to say it.

"This isn't why you're here, Willis. What aren't you telling me? Because what you told me so far feels like a program guide for an elementary school Christmas musical. So, spit it out, man."

I flinched as a shard of glass migrated to a new, yet to be discovered region of my back. Willis noticed it and commented that I hadn't moved the entire time he spoke. I gave a grunt and abbreviated situation report on my medical status.

When I turned my attention back to his briefing, he instead instructed me to cross my arms over my chest. He moved behind me while I struggled to do as he said, "Jesus, Otto. Is it really that bad?" Too busy biting back pain to answer; I continued my fight to cross my arms.

I wasn't even sure why I trusted him. But at this point if someone told me that sticking needles in my eyes would ease the pain, I would happily slam said eye onto a fully loaded pincushion. He reached over my shoulders and finished my task for me. Then, in one smooth movement, he kneeled, pinned my arms to my chest with his arms, pulled me in close, and stood straight up, taking me with him.

My feet left the floor as my spine emitted a sound akin to a roll of bubble-wrap being crushed. Vertebrae snapped into alignment one after another like a zipper running the length of my back. The pain the sudden movement caused was replaced with relief like I had never experienced.

After my feet touched down, two things happened: The relief *almost* made me cry. And I headed to the bathroom.

"Pick up the seat, Otto. This isn't a frat-house."

"Natalia, I'm not seven years old, I got it covered," I responded to my sister-in-law who had obviously been eavesdropping.

I rejoined Willis, thanked him, and asked, "What just happened? I was practically crippled just seconds ago."

I'm still unsure if Willis' answer was a dig or the truth, I'm a little sensitive about getting old. He said, "I've seen it dozens of times. People with soft-cores or weaker mid-sections have issues with spinal alignment. When you're out of alignment, it causes a host of issues. So, tighten up, Otto or you'll find yourself jammed up while in a fight. And that'll only end one way."

So, Willis called me *soft* AND *weak* in one sentence. Annoyed, embarrassed, and a little pissed, I told Willis to finish. I remained standing… because I could!

He moved through the information efficiently and with clarity designed for a kindergartner. "Otto, I don't have time for everything, but I'll come back after the VP's visit. Know this: RAM wants to expand the MST program and we can't let that happen. Start thinking about how we shut it down. That's all."

Preparing to leave, Willis said, "One last thing, we're transporting two of your wounded to St. Joe's hospital. Lewis told me about a conversation with the most terrifying person he's ever talked to. It was supposed to happen after the VP's visit, but we're bending the order to fit the need. Also, Andy's blood will be tested. I can say I've seen nothing like what Andy's experiencing. I'm curious to see what his deal is."

Willis, the rat-bastard, had just turned the tables on me. I somehow felt guilty for being mad when I had every right to be mad. He's a sneaky one that Willis. "Hey… thanks for taking care of our people." With a nod, Willis exited the house. Now I stood alone in a strange house debating my next move.

Stevenson radioed Willis as he was en route to meet them, "Time to rally-up, Sergeant, we have some very sick people onboard."

Willis responded, "I have you in sight. Let's get them to the hospital."

"Copy that. How'd it go with Otto?"

"He's mad, but he's a patriot. He'll get over it." Willis realized he'd eventually need to tell Lewis and Stevenson about trying to limit the MST program, just not today.

"Natalia, I'm going to help with the fence. Tell Darline, since you've been on the radio with her the entire time Willis was here, that I'll be late."

I exited the house and radioed Lisa from the front yard.

"What's up, Mr. Van Winkle?"

"Meet me at the main gate. Time to talk about the MST program." I shut the radio off, avoiding any sharp-tongued retorts from the devil-woman, and limped towards the main gate.

Chapter 39
Going Yard

Randy's AR belched a never-ending string of copper-jacketed death as he covered the team's left-flank. The UC herd had materialized from the wooded area bordering the south fence of the construction yard. Access to the yard was gained via a section of fence someone had cut through since Jay's last visit.

They had just finished loading supplies onto the flatbed of the tractor trailer when Steve Waters was dragged down by the initial pair of monsters drawn to the activity. His screams sent the entire team in his direction, but he was already lost. The UC kneeled over his body while taking it apart like butchers dressing a pig.

The stench of intestinal fluid swirling with death's reek overpowered the team, forcing a hard stop fifteen feet from the attack. These UC showed an accelerated amount of decomposition. Their clothing was a mess of torn fabric covered in mud and human gore as graying skin stretched over bone belied the illusion of living beings.

The progression of decay did not escape Randy or Stone's attention. "How are they still able to move? The laws of nature say this is impossible!" Stone yelled.

As if in response, Steve's head suddenly flopped in their direction and seemed to cast an accusatory glare on Stone; he raised his Tavor and ended the grotesque banquet.

After Stone closed *Steve's Deli*, Randy took his current position atop one of the two dump trucks the team needed to secure. It afforded him clear firing lines for the entire one-fifty by fifty yard area comprising the equipment storage enclosure. Secured by six-foot-high, barbed-wire-topped chain-linked fencing, the interior was stacked high with all manner of construction essentials. A hard-used shed housing small hand tools was centrally positioned on the yard's perimeter. Randy was determined to secure the area for future use, but first he needed to ensure they made it home without losing another life.

The rest of the UCs spotted the opening and poured through. Within seconds the enclosure's dead population numbered over thirty.

The remaining team consisted of Jay, Randy, Stone, Jack, and Arthur. Each scrambled to complete their assigned task while trying to avoid becoming a UC meal.

"We have to go!" Stone yelled to Jay as he attempted to empty the 57-Stone occupying the truck beds. "Leave the gravel in the dump trucks and get the semi moving. I'll drive this dump. Jack, you drive the other. Randy, Arthur, cut a path for us!"

Arthur climbed into the Hummer parked next to Randy's position and brought it online. Stone shouldered his Tavor to provide cover for Jack as he zigzagged to his assigned truck. But Jack didn't need help. His M&P barked during his entire trek; unfortunately he only managed kill shots on fifty percent of his targets. As Stone entered the dump's cab, he realized he needed to work with the eldest Hammer on his shooting.

Jay signaled to Stone, through the windshield, to pick up the CB radio. "I'm planning on plowing through the monsters blocking the gate. Stay on my tail. The Hummer should bring up the rear."

Jay slid the semi into gear and proceeded to the exit. Stone slapped the outside of the cab signaling Randy they would be moving, prompting Randy to dismount and join Arthur. Stone yelled to Randy that the Hummer would provide cover on their six. Jay would cut the path.

A moment later, Jay slammed into half a dozen monsters blocking the gate, leaving bloody smears in his wake. Stone now understood why Otto wanted the trucks; the community was going medieval on UC threats… Stone smiled his approval as the team raced home.

Chapter 40
Coming In Hot

Slowed by my protesting and angry body, I took forever to reach the main gate. Lisa had already arrived and carried on a conversation with Tesha.

The days were growing increasingly hot and sticky as the height of summer arrived. Our teams working the fence were glistening with sweat as they labored to secure our future.

The heat reminded me of summertime as a tween. I'd spend entire days exploring our neighborhood on my bicycle and getting home in time to catch Dad pulling some form of barbequed meat from the grill. I remembered hording firecrackers, against Dad's orders, to celebrate the 4th of July. The thought stopped me mid-step; I realized I had missed Independence Day. My favorite holiday, the only holiday that matters. It had zipped by without a single celebratory sparkler being lit, ribs being grilled, or cold beer being shared with a neighbor!

"CRAP." My outburst garnered the attention of the anxious security teams guarding the group working on the fence.

Raising my hands in mock surrender, I said, "Sorry, people. I lost control for a second. Nothing to see here. Carry on."

Lisa, of course, commented, "Otto, you just *now* lost control and for only a second? I call bullshit. You've never had control over your faculties, that's why people only tolerate you. They think you're impaired and feel sorry for you."

Lisa makes me want to scream obscenities at the sky.

I ignored her and said, "Tesha, good to see you. How's the little guy?" I hadn't taken Lisa's bait, causing her to throw a puzzled look at me and forcing a wry smile to break on Tesha's glistening, dirt-smudged face.

"Back at you, sir. Devon's well, Mr. Otto. But, like most, he's confused that dead people don't stay dead."

I detected Lisa inching closer, so I braced for her *flinch move*. I figured she had bragged to Tesha about her sucker-punch and my resulting black eye. Now she wanted to demonstrate her *control* over me. *Not today, she-devil, not today!*

"Well, Tesha, I can't say I blame him. The world makes no sense at all. Like, for instance, Lisa trying to sneak up on me and play the *made you flinch* game. She resembles a playground bully trying to extort a nickel from the sick kid. It is, as they say, nonsensical."

Lisa appeared caught in mid-flinch mode: arms up, stepping towards me, and a wicked grin lighting up her demonic features.

"Hello, Lisa. Is that your rotten soul I smell in the air?" It was an excellent burn, except something actually smelled rotten.

"Dillan, you smell that?" I yelled to the young man working dangerously exposed thirty feet outside the fence.

Dillan stood flagpole straight, sniffing the air. We both recognized the sound of a rumbling diesel engine the same instant one of our platform guards called out a warning of a vehicle approaching from the northeast. Shit, that wasn't the direction our team would travel home from.

Lisa grabbed her radio when it squelched to life, and Jay's voice broke. "We're on our way home. We lost St—."

His broadcast ended and I lost my mind. I screamed into my radio, ordering Jay to finish his message. Nothing! Lisa reached over and turned my radio on.

I forgot I had shut it off after telling her to join me at the fence. I didn't look up or thank her. She was the reason I'd turned it off, so no thank you for her. I pressed the talk button and screamed for Jay to finish his transmission. Again, the radio was silent. "No, no, no this isn't happening. God, please not this."

I put my panic attack on hold when the platform guard identified the vehicle as an *all-black, military-style troop carrier. A quarter mile out and closing fast.*

Dillan kicked into overdrive, barking orders at a pace matching a machinegun's rate of fire. Twenty or so residents rushed towards the gate, each seeming to understand his or her responsibility in the face of an attack.

The engine grew louder as it rumbled in the community's direction. Dillan's voice broke over the radio asking them to identify themselves, knowing they wouldn't. We had already identified what was happening. We were being attacked again!

This time was different. We weren't the sheep they expected. The community was ready to fight!

I lost track of Dillan as the workers scrambled through the gate, taking up defensive positions along the fence.

"Dillan for Otto."

"Go for Otto."

Lisa stacked up next to me, her clenched fists and laser focus on my radio confirming that she was ready to exact revenge.

"Grab Lisa and join me. I'm still outside the fence. I have a plan."

We were on the move a moment later and secured the gate as we exited.

With only my XDm and no additional magazine, I was concerned they would overpower us in a direct confrontation. I hoped he wanted to go at them *Viet Cong* style!

"This is it; we make our stand now and we end them!" Dillan screamed. "Platforms, open fire as soon as the transport is in range. Everyone else, find your assigned location and you hold your ground no matter what you hear. Dillan, out!"

"Dillan, this is Kathy at the south fence. We have a troop carrier coming in hot. We will engage them in less than thirty seconds."

Dillan stuffed his anger and simply replied, "Fire at will."

Shots rang out simultaneously to our south and from the northeast corner as the battle commenced.

With a measured intensity, Dillan told us to follow him. He shared his plan as we headed east on an intercept course. My anger built while I struggled to keep pace with the younger duo. I used it to push my body past its breaking point. I would pay the price, if I lived.

Dillan yelled "NOW!" and the two of them split off, Lisa hard north as Dillan veered south. I continued on a course to intercept the enemy head-on.

Not five seconds later the transport came into view. It had taken heavy fire from the community and found cover alongside a house a block north of our home. The front of the troop carrier faced west, affording me a clear view of the damage it had sustained. The windshield was spider-webbed from dozens of rounds intended for the enemy within. Blood covered the passenger-side interior and the door hung half open, confirming our enemy had been reduced by one. Tendrils of steam wisped from the grill as the front driver's-side tire hissed its last breath.

I took cover under the sagging branches of a mature pine tree situated twenty feet from the crippled vehicle. It afforded excellent lines of fire should anyone attempt to exit the cab.

The troop carrier was an old school deuce-and-a-half, modified with a hardtop covering the cargo area. It sported matte-black paint void of identifying marks. Definitely not RAM military property.

The stench was overwhelming, but not strong enough to carry for miles, meaning we had another problem to solve. I heard the moans of the dead the same instant the driver's door swung open. I press-checked my XDm. Satisfied with the results, I placed the sights on the head of the soldier. Suddenly the driver fell to his knees then hard on his face. After detecting no movement in the cab, I radioed Dillan and Lisa with an update. "Possibly two down; I see no additional living. I think the cargo-hold is full of UCs. Follow the steam and the stench, I'll be waiting."

The sounds of battle raged from the south fence line as the community defended itself from the secondary attack. I worried that it had gone sideways for us as I cleared the cab. I pulled the passenger door completely open and found an empty blood-stained seat. I figured the passenger took heavy damage and bailed. I started to follow the blood trail when the sound of a slide racking next to my head enraged me. *You must be the missing passenger!*

"Don't be a dumbass, son. You're wounded, you've lost your transport, and you're dealing with a nasty old man. Put the gun down."

A moment later, Lisa's voice sounded to my left, "The nasty old man told you to drop your gun."

I turned to see Lisa holding her Glock 17 against the temple of the helmeted combatant.

Lisa was forced to disarm the stubborn, non-verbal soldier. She stepped back two feet and stuffed the gun in her left cargo pocket. When she ordered the soldier to his knees, he launched in her direction while unsheathing a knife from under his tactical vest. Lisa cut the attack short with one round to his head.

"You stupid son-of-a-bitch! Why did you do that?" Lisa ranted while she kicked the downed soldier to confirm he was dead.

Dillan appeared from behind the transport, pistol raised and eyes focused on the aftermath of Lisa's decisive action.

"Clear!" I yelled, prompting Dillan to holster his weapon. Lisa bent to inspect the body for useful items or INTEL when our radios came to life.

"We need reinforcements at the south fence. NOW!"

Chapter 41
Brush

Jay tossed his handheld radio to the passenger seat and grabbed the more powerful CB. Each of his trucks was equipped with one and he hoped the CB's frequency wasn't affected by the interference. He called out for anyone in the convoy to answer.

A static-filled voice responded, "This is Jack. What happened, Jay? Your transmission dropped mid-sentence; now I'm unable to raise anyone."

Stone grabbed the CB in his truck, "This is Stone. I think I just spotted the reason for the interference. Continue home, I'll flag down Randy and Arthur. Stone, out."

He activated the dump truck's hazards to warn Randy he was slowing. A flash later, the Hummer sat next to him on the narrow street. Randy was only able to slide his window down an inch before it screeched to a halt. With face red and bulging veins, Randy yelled, "What?"

"Act natural, Randy. I spotted a black Hummer in our shadow. I'm betting a crisp Franklin they're behind the attack, the jamming of the handheld radios, or both. We need to end this bullshit, now."

The suspicious Hummer sat fifty feet away concealed behind a six-foot-high partially burned brush pile on the north side of the road. It faced away from the street, presenting its windowless sloped back to the passing convoy. Stone was tipped off by a glint of sunlight off the driver's-side-view mirror as they roared home.

Other than the mirror, it blended in perfectly with the blackened plant material.

"When I tell you to, pull in front of me. I'm going to test Otto's plan for the trucks on some metal." Stone placed the massive International 4300 DT-466 in neutral and monitored the brush pile for movement. After a quick ten-count he committed to his plan. "NOW!" he yelled, turning the wheel hard while grinding the behemoth into reverse and pinning the gas-pedal to the floor.

The truck lurched and strained against its massive weight as Stone angled it toward his target. Gravel leaped from the bed as it left pavement and contacted sod but remained on target like a monstrous guided missile. Stone couldn't see the Hummer's occupants but imagined the looks of surprise and terror when reality, in the shape of his truck, hit them.

The standard-issue Hummer proved no match against the fully burdened International 4300 and the brush pile offered no protection from the leading edge of the dump's bed. It exploded through the weak camouflage, nearly shearing the Hummer's roof off as the force flipped it on its side.

Randy and Arthur pulled their Hummer alongside the wreckage. Arthur provided cover as Randy and Stone converged on the devastated hulk. Rifles shouldered, they ordered the occupants to exit. Nothing moved. Again they barked urgently for the enemy to exit. Their orders again went unanswered.

Stone announced, "I'm going to search it. Cover me."

Randy adjusted his position, affording him a clear view of both Stone and the Hummer. "Make it quick, I'm sure UCs from miles away heard that."

"Got it!" Stone stuck his head through the half-open door. "Clear. I have two dead. Help me pull them out."

Randy said, "Arthur, cover us. If the wind even blows funny, let us know."

Arthur took a sentry position between their Hummer and the enemy's. Randy and Stone removed the passenger first. His blood-soaked face flopped at an unnatural left-slant with his nose flush against his shoulder. Two minutes later, both heavily damaged bodies lay side-by-side as Randy and Stone searched for information that might explain their actions against the group.

Randy checked both weapons he'd pulled from the wreck. "Empty. Not a single round in either." Holding up a mangled hunk of electronics, he said, "I'm guessing this little ditty is a signal jamming device." He secured everything in their Hummer then tried his radio. "Randy for Jay or Jack."

Jack's voice burst from the speaker, "Where the hell are you? Oh, and apparently the radios work again."

Randy asked, "Are you in radio range of home?"

Jay answered, "Close enough. We will contact them and report back."

"Copy that, Jay. Randy, out."

Stone scanned the dead men's IDs and shook his head. "They're kids. Seventeen and twenty. Problem is they're from BSU." The reality jolted him. "We need to go, NOW."

Chapter 42
Clearing a Path

Jay radioed Dillan and gave him their ETA. A response plagued by static chopped back. "We're... attack... need..." Then silence.

"Jack, press your foot to the floor."

Both vehicles belched black smoke as their powerful engines responded to the flood of diesel into their cylinders.

Randy slammed the door to the Hummer as Jay broke over the radio, "Randy, do you copy?"

The stress in Jay's voice caused Randy to break into a cold sweat. "Talk to me, Jay." Through a static-filled line, Randy heard three words, "Home... under... attack."

"Drive it like you stole it, Arthur."

Randy was pinned back as Arthur pushed the Hummer to its limit. "Stone, did you have a good copy on Jay?"

"Yes! Stand on your gas pedal; I'll push this beast as hard as I can. Do not wait on me."

A ten-count later and a hard message was conveyed by Stone, "Kill anyone you don't recognize."

That's it; we've reached that point already. Randy made a note to ask Otto how quickly this happened in his zombie books.

Thinking of Otto forced an unguarded moment from Randy. "God, please let him be inside the gate. He's my best friend, and he's slow as shit." Arthur looked a question at Randy. Surprised that he'd verbalized his thought, he simply said, "Have you ever seen Otto run? If you have, you'll know why I'm praying for him."

Lisa and Dillan were moving before the south fence ended its transmission. Torn between ending the UC threat stowed in the troop carrier's cargo hold, radioing Jay, or joining Lisa and Dillan in reinforcing the south fence, I wobbled back and forth: step, stop, step, stop… I looked like a squirrel crossing a busy street. Finally I yelled out, "Do not wait for me." Not that they had. They were already twenty-five yards away and not looking back.

I could hear the firefight in the distance and realized I needed to hurry. The UC payload had whipped into a lather, rocking the transport on its springs. Decision made. I needed to deal with the deadly cargo.

I checked the cab for weapons and found two old, beat-up M16 rifles between the seats. "This should do the trick." I pressed the mag-release and discovered an empty magazine. Frustrated, I pulled the charging handle and found the chamber empty. "Useless and filthy, just like your country!" I yelled at the dead BSU soldiers as I slammed the worthless weapon to the ground. I checked the second M16. Also empty!

"How did your government expect you to fight? They didn't, you're expected to die. Well, *mission accomplished!*"

Panic and anger seized control as I stomped to the back of the transport and pulled the tarp back. The sight that greeted me forced me into an involuntary retreat and I drew my XDm.

Eleven UCs stood chained together, forming two rows facing the cab with their backs to the exit. They'd secured the chains with two massive padlocks positioned at the end of the cargo hold's floor. I surmised they'd planned to unload the monsters by removing the locks and driving forward, forcing the now unsecured UCs to free fall from the opening.

My XDm holds thirteen rounds plus one in the pipe. I had eleven monsters to dispatch. The numbers worked. After eleven strokes of the trigger, the deadly cargo was silent but still dangerous. Through hundreds of buzzing flies, I noticed the UC closest to me had a thin steel-cable running from its side, which attached to the metal framing supporting the modified cover. Following the string to its point of attachment on the UC exposed the truth. They had planned to set another *suicide* UC loose on our home. It also confirmed how close I had come to killing myself. An errant round or hard tug from the UC could have triggered the timer on the explosives, sending me to my death in a mix of zombie parts and fire.

I shook off my daze and killed two birds with one stone. I moved my damaged body towards the battle at our south fence while radioing Jay. "Jay, Randy... Stone. Someone, please respond."

A voice broke through, causing my heart to race. "We need you, Otto. They let the cargo loose back here and we're trapped outside the fence." It was Dillan, and he sounded frantic.

"I'm coming! Hold the line, Dillan."

A slow jog was all my dented body allowed. When I arrived, my blood went white-hot. Lisa and Dillan held two BSU soldiers at gunpoint against their large transport while a hailstorm of bullets ripped through the attacking UCs just twenty yards away. This transport dwarfed the other one. Its size allowed it to unleash twice the number of UCs on our home.

I approached Dillan and Lisa as they screamed at the soldiers for information. After finding the rigged UC aboard the other carrier, I understood that at least one of these UCs was a shambling bomb!

"Are they talking?" I asked.

Lisa barked, "Not a word, Otto. And this one, with the smug grin, is going to get his ass kicked."

I stepped next to the smug soldier and placed my gun against his temple. The smile remained on his grime-streaked face.

"Which one is strapped with explosives?"

The smile faltered but returned.

"Which one?" I growled.

Still nothing.

"WHICH ONE?"

A snorting laugh was his reply.

The blood from his head sprayed the second soldier's face, transforming the man into a babbling fool.

A sharp blow from Dillan focused the soldier's thoughts.

"Orange sweater, she's wearing a bright orange sweater."

"Lisa, kill him, lock him up, I don't care. I'll be back in a minute."

I had noticed the UC in question in the ankle-deep field grass ten feet from the pavement when I arrived on scene. So I headed in that direction. Mrs. Orange Sweater had stayed on course!

I probably should have called a ceasefire, but I didn't, and I found myself on the battlefield before my head registered I had even moved.

The gunfire stopped as our community took notice of my boneheaded move. Someone called me an idiot. It may have been Darline. "Idiot on the move, idiot trying to *save you*," I snapped. *I'll pay for that later.*

When the gunfire stopped, so did the UC, as if confused by the sudden silence. My opportunity was now. My brain ordered my legs to run, but my legs told my brain NO. So I continued to step-hop-jog to intercept the walking bomb.

All of a sudden, a skinny human form blurred passed on my right. I flinched and brought my pistol to bear. A millisecond from pulling the trigger and the blur became clear. Lisa was moving on the target. I almost shot her! The realization scared the shit out of me. I wouldn't share that with her. I don't want her thinking we're all *buddy buddy.*

As she closed on the terrorist UC, she let loose a war cry that would have frozen a battle-hardened soldier in fear. It held rage, anger, and determination, the depth of which I had never witnessed. Lisa thrived in this environment. It gave her something to fight for, and she liked it! She was an asset. Someone our community saw as a leader. Someone I was starting to respect… *unless she punched me again.*

Our primary UC target turned toward the shrieking warrior and received a 9mm round to the forehead for her effort. As she crumbled to the ground, the explosive's tripwire flailed after her.

"Don't touch the wire, Lisa. It's the end of us if you do."

Lisa's momentum carried her past the UC lying flat on her back, the tripwire coiled around her body with its frayed end resting on her chest.

She turned to engage the fan club she had attracted. Raising her gun, she prepared to fire only to find the slide locked back. Empty! She searched frantically for her spare magazine but found empty pockets. She heaved the Glock at the closest UC and reached for the pistol she'd confiscated from the BSU soldier.

A quick press-check revealed it too was empty. " Otto, I'm out of ammo."

I had halved the distance to her position and willed my body to move faster. "Go left, Lisa. I don't have a clear shot. Do it, NOW." We were working ourselves into a huge jam.

The last ten UC had coalesced shoulder to shoulder and we had inadvertently positioned ourselves on either side of the deadly procession. The community couldn't fire on them due to the high probability we would get caught in the crossfire. Instead of firing, they began banging on the fence, screaming and doing anything to distract the UCs. It was no use; they had locked onto Lisa like a gang of blue-hairs at the early bird buffet.

Lisa broke left, toward the street and Dillan. I pulled the trigger twice, sending two stank-asses to the ground. That's when my slide locked back. I didn't bother searching for another magazine. I didn't have one. Unlike Lisa, I holstered my gun (I love my XDm) and followed her lead.

She ran wide left and with the two UCs I had put down, she would easily clear the UC line. I, on the other hand, was quickly getting flanked. The UCs had formed a "U" and started tightening it from a capital "U" to a lowercase "u" with me in the middle. I again willed my body to move, but the twisted brush grabbed my left foot and sent me to the ground. Classic face-plant! Why do I always end up on the damn ground?

Head spinning from my hard landing, I got to a kneeling position and something dawned on me. The UCs weren't rasping. They hadn't uttered a sound. Was this evolutionary or was I giving them too much credit, projecting cognizant rationale onto mindless eating machines? "It doesn't matter, dumbass. Getting to your feet matters. Stand, Otto. If you don't, you'll die."

Lisa cut my self-admonishment short when she materialized an inch from my face. "Hold on, Otto."

I thought it an odd direction. Hold on to what and why did I need to hold on to it?

She got behind me, grabbed me under my shoulders, and pulled. Got it. She'd just saved me again.

Heels dragging through soft earth, I had a perfect view of the situation she had saved me from. The UCs had closed to within a couple of feet of me before she dragged me away.

I watched as the confused UCs adjusted their pursuit in our direction. Suddenly the air was filled by the growl of a large engine followed by an air-horn blasting. Then the UCs vanished in a slurry of body-parts and blood. The space the UCs had occupied was now filled by an enormous dump truck.

Body parts and gravel pelted me as I covered my face lest it sustain even more damage. Lisa stopped pulling, so I used her as leverage and stood. I turned to face her. Short on words, I hugged her. "Thank you, Lisa. That's twice."

Lisa didn't return my hug and pushed me away. "Personal space, Otto. You're in my personal space." She had a hard edge to her voice, but her eyes were moist.

"Awww, you care about me, Lisa. You're like a little sister. A little sister craving the acceptance of her big brother. Well, consider it done."

I'm not sure what about Lisa made me want to antagonize her. I'd intended to be nice, but my mouth wouldn't cooperate with my brain. She'd saved my life, and I wanted to thank her. But here we were.

The moisture in Lisas eye's evaporated like water on a hot frying pan. Eyes narrow, veins bulging, and face one shade past crimson, she reared back with her right fist. It was coming—another black eye. But the combination of another blast from an air-horn and Jack whooping from the cab interrupted her assault.

Jack pushed the door open and jumped to the ground. He was on me a second later. Hands on the sides of my face, he asked, "You okay, Otto?"

I nodded then he looked past me. "Lisa, thank you for saving my brother and for not punching him. He has that effect on people, so I know it took a bunch of self-control to stop yourself."

Caught off guard, because the only thing that kept me from collecting another black eye was Jack's interruption, not her self-control, Lisa gave a sheepish smile and nodded.

Dillan yelled, "Yo, heads up. Two UCs to your left."

No sooner had he finished than a barrage of gunfire from behind the fence finished the straggling UCs.

Dillan still held the BSU soldier at gunpoint. Frustrated that he couldn't join the fight because of his prisoner, he pistol-whipped the youngster, dropping him unconscious to the ground.

"Whoop, whoop, that's my husband driving that truck. Clear that path, baby!" Natalia screamed from the fence, turning Jack's cheeks rosy.

"Jack, I don't see the others. You're not the only one, are you?"

Jack's posture stiffened. "Steve was killed."

"Oh, thank God," I blurted out.

"What'd you say, Otto?" Lisa asked with a tilted head.

All eyes on me, I realized what I'd done. I'd cheered the death of one man over another. Some people might find it reprehensible, but I wasn't about to apologize.

"Well, Sis, I simply expressed relief that our brother is alive. I admit I could have found a better way to communicate my feelings, but I didn't."

Dillan asked, "Otto, did you call Lisa *sis?* As in *sister?*"

"I did. She wants to be my sister, she just won't admit it. Tell 'em, Sis, you're now part of the Hammer clan."

I'm sure Lisa was going to respond by opening a can of whoop-ass on me. But our radios crackling to life saved me. "This is the main gate. I've got a big-rig entering."

I faced Jack. "Stone, Randy. Where are they, Jack?"

My brother swallowed hard. "They stayed behind to deal with more of these idiots," he said while kicking the downed soldier.

I bent down and grabbed the BSU soldier. "Someone help me load him into the transport. He's going to answer my questions before we turn him over to Willis. He better pray our people are alive."

We had just passed through the east gate when the main gate radioed again. "Additional vehicles entering the main gate. We've lost one."

The dazed BSU soldier sat next to Lisa in the back seat as the main gate ended its transmission; she slammed his semiconscious head off the window.

"After we get checked, I'm going to have a talk with you. And I'm bringing my brother!"

CHAPTER 43
WICKED WEB

Shafter sat on his crumpled bed sheets reviewing his notes from yesterday's meeting. They held the same information as the notes from every other damn meeting they'd had since he'd arrived. The realization that the Coalition had no plan to regain control crushed him. The only thing they'd managed to accomplish was organizing meeting after meeting after meeting. Pathetic!

"Today is the day I take control of this unorganized group and turn them into a slick political machine! We need leadership, my leadership, to regain our power. No longer will I suffer the indignity of acting as the meeting scribe."

Emboldened by his proclamation, he scurried to the bathroom and prepared for a shower. He glared at the faucet, "Will you bring me water today, or will you again spit acrid mud at me?"

The Sea Cliff was once a magnificent hotel. Located on the top floor, his suite came equipped with every modern amenity he deserved. But they had no housekeeping, no maintenance to speak of, and no aides to assist them. The military force protecting them was a cobbled-together jumble of angry children more interested in disobeying the Coalition than protecting it. The conditions were virtually prehistoric!

He grabbed the faucet handle, said a prayer, and turned it to full-hot. For a long ten-count, nothing happened. Clanging pipes signaled his prayer was not answered. He attempted to close the valve and was rewarded with brown, abhorrent-smelling "water" splashing along his arm.

In his previous life, the life he deserved, he would have raged against hotel management for such an incident. Today, he managed only a whimper of defeat. RAM caused this; RAM was the reason he was living in conditions well below his status in life. *RAM will pay for this!*

Shafter retrieved a soiled bath towel from the mound in the corner. He scrubbed at the filth, but the smell won out. He searched for a bottle of water but found only empty containers littering his suite. "I shouldn't have used my rations to water-down my Scotch."

Still scrubbing at the offending stench, he scowled as his room phone buzzed. The only functioning amenity in his suite, other than sporadic electricity, was the phone. The only person who ever called him was that shill, Piles.

"We have no water for bathing. What are you doing about it?"

A sound similar to oysters being shucked greeted him as Piles cleared her throat, signaling disapproval of his tone.

"Scribe Shafter, you will join the Coalition in the main ballroom immediately."

Pushed past the edge by the insult, Shafter replied, "You stretched-face drunk, who do yo—." His retaliation was cut short by a cackling Piles slamming her phone onto its cradle.

Shafter walked to the staircase that would take him to the Main Ballroom. A glance out the windows lining the hallway proved the situation hadn't improved. The children still manned the hastily erected fence. The boys and girls along the perimeter, armed with sticks, clubs, and knives culled the random monsters congregating along the fence line.

Firearms were only issued to the Coalition's security detail. The soldiers had attempted to distribute guns to the members of the Coalition, but they held a vote and defeated the proposal.

"We employ lackeys to handle guns, to protect us," Senator Finkelstein proclaimed with exuberance after the vote. Their only accomplishment to date.

Shafter entered the ballroom and found Piles, Finkelstein, and Cortina seated next to one another at the largest table in the room. A chair opposite their position sat pulled away from the table. A notepad, pen, and a glass of water on the table in front of the chair. He stared, incredulous, at the setting.

"Sit, sit, Scribe. We need to begin our daily business. Speaking of which, we'll need your phone. NOW, thank you."

Still standing, rubbing his temples, his frustration on display, he answered, "Senator Piles, my deepest apologies; I failed to secure it upon exiting my quarters. Perhaps had I been able to shower, as it appears all of you were, I would have been more alert."

Finkelstein slammed her hand on the table. "Enough of your insubordination, Scribe Shafter. Where is your phone? Oh, never mind, Senator Piles will call it now to help determine its current location."

"NO, err, reason for the effort, honorable Senator. I'll retrieve it during lunch." The stench caused by the acrid mud on his arm increased as sweat oozed from his pores.

"No need," Piles said as she dialed her sat-phone. She engaged the speaker function and waited as the phone connected to the number.

A supremely confident voice answered, "Well, to whom am I speaking?"

"So sorry, wrong number," Piles screeched and disconnected the call.

"Why did you speak? Like, that voice of yours is, like, a neon sign identifying its owner. Like, show some self control," Cortina admonished her cohort while up talking and drawing out the vowels in every word she spoke.

Piles glared at the youthful woman. Then, without warning, she launched her heavy water glass, striking Cortina on the bridge of her nose. The crunching of bone and gushing of blood shocked the room as Senator Cortina shrieked.

"Oh, so sorry, dear. It slipped from my grasp. Please, excuse yourself and tend to that awful mess on your face. Don't fret, we'll continue without you." Piles smirked.

Senator Cortina shot from her chair, rushing the hagfish from California. She realized her mistake far too late. She had underestimated Piles' ruthlessness, her willingness to do anything to retain her power. The fork was entering her right eye when those truths revealed themselves. She crumpled to the floor, lifeless, a moment later.

"Well, I must have forgotten about the fork in my hand. Poor thing. God bless her heart. She held a bright political future once we overthrow RAM."

Shafter understood the true meaning. The purge had begun. His mind slammed into overdrive, scrambling for words that would buy him time. Time to plan his escape. Instead, it told him he would be dying today. Strange; he found comfort in death's realization. An understanding that death brings peace. "Peace, what's that?"

"Excuse me, Scribe Shafter; do you have something to share?" The question startled him. he hadn't intended to orate his thought.

Finkelstein was far too calm considering the chaos of the moment. She asked again, "Something to share?"

Shafter chugged his glass of water; he held the glass tight while waiting to be attacked. "I'm suddenly feeling ill. I should adjourn to my quarters. My apologies, Senators." He shuffled backwards towards the door while speaking, never taking his eyes off the murderous duo.

Well, this explained why Finkelstein was so adamant about banning Coalition members from possessing firearms. He was defenseless, except for his *assault*-water glass, that is.

Just as he reached the exit, Piles asked, "So, what to do about your phone? You recognized the voice, did you not?"

He had, and he understood their plan had just collapsed around them.

"The better question, Senator Piles, is what to do with the murdered body of a sitting member of BSU Senate. Don't you think?" His question incited cackling fits of laughter from the duo.

"Dear, dear Scribe Shafter, have you been paying attention at all? Maybe you haven't. Let me enlighten you," Finkelstein cooed. "The old world is dead. People eat one another. The dead don't stay dead. Our beautiful BSU is uninhabitable." Her effectual pause seemed never-ending. "We're all that remains of the power structure. So, by default, we operate free of societal norms or restrictions. In summation, we do as we please or, if you will, as we see fit to ensure the power structure survives. This includes breaking some eggs to create a better omelet. Please, take heed, good sir."

The prospect of unchallenged power triggered a response akin to mainlining heroin. The visualization caused his eyes to glaze and mouth to gape. Drool on his chin brought him back to reality. He reminded himself that he was no longer an element in the structure Finkelstein spoke of. Her threat made that clear. His usefulness had vanished the second Piles called the satellite phone he'd lost evacuating the camp in Buffalo.

"Sounds like utopia. Nevertheless, I feel unwell. I'll attempt to join you for dinner. Till then, Senators, I bid you a good day."

As Shafter departed the ballroom, Piles and Finkelstein erupted in laughter. Piles retrieved the walkie-talkie *thingy* from her briefcase. "Senator Piles calling Sergeant… what's-your-face. Shafter is heading home. Report back in fifteen."

Shafter started with a walking pace and ended in a flat-out run as he slammed into the door of his room. He would lock himself down and develop a strategy.

Bursting into his room, he slammed the door and engaged the deadbolt. Not satisfied, he wedged the desk chair from his workstation under the door handle. *That should hold, for now.*

"Thank you, Senator. I'm sorry, Scribe Shafter. I was worried about how I would stop you from exiting the room."

Shafter's heart seemed to stop upon hearing the voice in his room.

"Seems you're tangled in your own wicked web."

Shafter couldn't find the courage to face the voice; his body slumped in resignation as he prepared to die.

"Don't worry, it'll be over soon."

Chapter 44
Best Laid Plans

Piles' security guard led the way back to her suite, the largest the hotel offered. She felt intoxicated from the afternoon's events. *GOD, I'm amazing. Invincible better describes the sensation!* Soon, she'd feel this way every day.

She just needed to establish contact with the DPRK and activate phase two. Then, she would watch RAM fall to DPRK's invasion force. After which, they'd create a Zombie Cleanup Committee utilizing RAM's resources to eliminate the infected from RAM and away from its beautiful border walls.

Clearing RAM would be more complicated than anticipated thanks to DPRK's shoddy testing and poor execution. *Not to worry. I'll have the machines, time, and expendable human equity to accomplish the task.*

The DPRK would be burdened with clearing BSU of infected. For their troubles, *Dear Leader* would be able to claim BSU as his. She knew Mr. Kim only wanted control over their nuclear reactors. "Joke's on you, little man. We decommissioned them a year ago. Every piece of technology was removed or destroyed. Have fun running around those empty shells."

Her security guard turned to face her and said, "I'm sorry Senator Piles, I didn't catch what you said."

Caught off guard, she snapped, "That, soldier man, is because you weren't supposed to. Now stop eavesdropping and mush." Her liver-spotted hand made a whipping motion.

Her guard bristled and thought about smashing the stock of his rifle into the vampire's mouth. But the piercing sound of her sat-phone broke his reverie and pulled him from his dream.

Piles fumbled through her briefcase in search of the ringing phone. The soldier noticed no less than three phones tumbling around as she groped the contents of her bag. *What the hell? Why three phones during the apocalypse? Who's getting cell service?* He averted his eyes when Piles glanced up at him, holding a large phone in a style he had never seen.

Piles didn't recognize the number, but the country code was unmistakable. The DPRK had found her!

"Get me to my room, NOW!" she hissed.

"You're three steps away. Get yourself to your room," he said and left her standing in the hallway, wide-eyed and alone. At that moment, he realized something. A select few, including him, held the power. These idiots couldn't defend themselves.

As he walked away, he yelled, "You're fired, Senator Leather Face."

Torn between reaming the soldier and answering the call, she decided on the latter.

"This is Senator Piles. To whom am I speaking?" She slithered into her suite as she waited for a response.

"Senator, all communication stopped with idiot Shafter. What happen?"

"I'll ask again, to whom am I speaking?"

"This FVC Choke. I no time…." Static spit from the speaker. "You need to know some… Dear Leader gone… plan change."

"WHAT ARE YOU SAYING? You're breaking up; repeat the message."

The line cleared enough to make Piles gag on the message.

"VC Packet in control. I change plan. We take everything from imperialist maggots. See you soon."

The call disconnected the same time her knees buckled. Her head was spinning as she searched for answers. A way to gain leverage over Packet, a man she knew well. A sadistic fiend of a man.

Still holding the phone, she scrolled through the previous calls until she found the number. She held her breath as the phone connected.

"Which treasonous hack am I speaking to?"

"Mr. Mallet, this is Senator Piles. I need to talk to you."

"Save your breath. You'll need it when you look out your window. We're happy to announce that the Coast Guard is back online."

Piles struggled to her feet and rushed to the window. Her room afforded her an impressive view of Lake Erie, one she had loved until now. The Coast Guard Heritage-class Offshore Patrol Cutter now ruined her picturesque vistas. Its 57mm gun tracked in the hotel's direction as men boarded a small black helicopter perched on the ship's helipad.

"Piles, please share this with Finkelstein. RAM has stopped taking prisoners."

Chapter 45
Town Hall

The restrained BSU soldier sat on the bench across from me as we waited to clear security. People were talking, but I didn't hear their words as I glared at our prisoner. I wanted to throat-punch him and watch him choke out of this world. A push on my side drew my attention to Lisa, who sat next to me.

She leaned in. "You did what you needed to; you saved lives today."

"Thanks, Lisa. Actually, I'm thinking about killing our *guest* in a slow and painful way." I leaned across the narrow aisle and stage-whispered, "Want to hear my plan? It's extremely detailed. Want me to share?"

The youngster's bulging eyes went bleary. His head thrashed side-to-side as he worked the restraints, attempting to flee.

Lisa smiled. "Well, I'd like to hear. What's the plan, Otto?"

I sat back. "You'll love it, Lisa. Remember how we talked about bayonet training, but we didn't have the resources to practice on?" We hadn't talked about it and we don't use bayonets, but the BSU soldier didn't know that.

Lisa's smile grew wicked. "I do, Otto, I do indeed remember. I like the direction you're headed. Please continue."

"I figured you'd approve. And, we just secured a *resource* for training. His screams should desensitize us to the brutality of running a human through with the blade; make it easier to disembowel his friends when we find the rat-bastards."

I screamed at the now hysterical soldier, "LISTEN TO ME. We lost a member of our community today. We almost lost many more. Another member's life is slipping away in a hospital bed lying next to another of our wounded friends." I realized that the security tent had gone silent. I didn't care.

"You will tell us why, and you will take us to your camp. When we're alone with you, rest assured you will tell us everything."

It took twenty minutes to complete our exams. When we exited the tent, the entire community awaited us. An eerie quiet gripped the crowd. Lisa, Dillan, and I shared determined stares with the men, women, and children of our home.

"Well, since we have all of you together, it's time to talk," I started. "Randy, Stone, Will, please join us. Al, please take the prisoner to one of the quarantine facilities. Keep him restrained and lock him in a bathroom, crawlspace, or a small hole in the ground."

I launched into my dialogue without waiting for the others to act on my requests. They already knew the truth.

"I need to tell you all something. It may be difficult to accept, but you need to hear it. Our mission to Entry Point One made something crystal clear. We are on the verge of losing everything to the virus. What we witnessed will change our approach to our safety. Each of us needs to take an active role in the preservation of this community and our lives."

I searched for the words I needed to drive home my message. "BSU has fallen. RAM's military has slaughtered thousands of people trying to enter our country. Our military is waging war at our border, a war that, if lost, means the end of RAM. As we left the area near the Entry Point, our military began bombardment of the area immediately outside of the wall."

The faces staring back at me turned hard. Guns were gripped by some as others pulled loved ones close. Resolve washed over the people of our community. They were ready to fight to keep our home safe, ready to fight to live.

"Today we will begin to strengthen OUR border and OUR home. Each of you will be called upon, each of you will contribute, each of you is essential to our survival. Dillan will organize us into teams that will be responsible for essential duties such as manufacturing ammunition, strengthening the fence, and conducting scavenging missions. We're going to utilize any skill you have for our survival."

I met the stare of the people who call this place home; the fire in their eyes told me we had a chance. "As many of you know, we've lost two friends. We need to ensure their deaths weren't in vain. They died for this country and this community. I promise you we will take our pound of flesh from the people that attacked us."

"We will be visited by the Vice President later today. We will listen to what he has to say. But starting today, our home is the only thing that matters. Let's get to work!"

People volunteering to join the teams Dillan would be organizing immediately surrounded him. I searched for Darline among the faces in the crowd. She was standing with Kit, Natalia, and Nila, or as I now referred to them, *the mean wives club*.

All of them were armed and had been at the fence defending the community.

Darline had a look resembling pride as I approached her, something I'm not used to. "Hey chick, I'm still alive. No matter how hard I try to get myself killed, Lisa keeps getting in the way."

She wrapped her arms around me and said, "You need another shower. WOW."

"Oh babe, that's your breath blowing back into your face. But don't worry, I still love you." A sharp poke to my ribs meant she wouldn't put the smack-down on me in front of her *posse*. But I was on thin ice.

She went to her tiptoes to get close to my ear, "What you did to that soldier… are you okay?"

I whispered back, "I'm all good. I may need therapy in a few years, for that and everything else I've done. But now, this second, I'm good."

Darline pulled back and told the mean wives she'd meet them at Pat's in a few. She faced me and said, "Today you became a leader of this community. They watched you sacrifice your humanity for them, push your body past its limits, and put your life on the line for them. What you did will never be forgotten; you showed them what it will take to survive."

"Do you think they'll read about me in schoolbooks someday? Like Armstrong and Aldrin?"

Darline rolled her eyes and said, "I'm going to Pat's. Go do something useful."

Will called me over, holding his radio above his head. "Willis wants to talk to you."

I grabbed the radio, ready to blitz Willis with my thoughts. "This is Otto. Did you deliver our people to the hospital?"

"Well, that's a fine howdy-do, Otto. And yes, we got your people and Andy's blood sample to the hospital. Also, you need to say 'over.' You're getting a little sloppy with that. Over."

"We've been attacked again, Willis. We have one BSU prisoner. If you want him alive, you'll need to get here ASAP.

Lisa and I plan to question him. I can't make any promises on his condition after we finish." I paused but didn't say over because I wasn't done talking, and the *sloppy* comment riled me.

Willis started to talk, and I quickly said, "Hey, I didn't say over." Sometimes the little things give us joy. "Also, two UCs from the attack were rigged with explosives. So, unless you don't mind me owning military-grade high explosives, you'll need to disarm them. Over."

"Otto, do you have wounded or fatalities? Over."

"Other than my pride, no wounded or dead community members. Three BSU soldiers are dead. Over."

"That's a good copy! We'll pick up the prisoner and disable the explosive UCs before the VP arrives. Over."

"What's your timing, Willis? Lisa wants to start her conversation with our prisoner ASAP."

"VP visit is tonight at 1900 hours. But we'll arrive in two hours to secure the prisoner and disable the UC." He didn't say over, and he didn't speak for a long minute. "Otto, you and Lisa start your conversation. Please understand, I need him breathing when we arrive. Willis, out."

"Willis, I'm never saying *over* again."

Chapter 46
Talk

Pink mist and human particulates still hung thick in the air as Albright pressed the 9mm to Williams' temple. "I asked you for numbers, Williams. Not training level. What is the force size of Operation Move In, outside of Ohio? How many states is it operating in? Who ordered it and how do we stop it? Where are the BSU leaders hiding?"

Bantam's corpse lay crumpled on the floor at Williams' feet. *I'm sorry, Bantam.* His mind raced for an answer that would save him from Bantam's fate. He had already given Albright the Cleveland force size and locations. He expected they were already dead or would be soon now that RAM knew their locations.

They hadn't been resupplied in weeks and would be out of ammunition and medical supplies. They were so poorly trained that scavenging for supplies was out of the question. He was lucky they were able to function at all without him hovering over them barking step-by-step instructions.

"I told you, I DON'T KNOW. I commanded the Cleveland invasion." A sharp crack to his left eye sent him to the floor, next to Bantam's husk. *The same spot; he hits me in the same spot every time.*

"Bullshit! I'm a soldier, Williams, not some idiot politician." Hulking over Williams' unmoving form, he continued berating him. "You had contact with other units; you had contact with boots on the ground. Hell, you probably sat in the planning meetings when this twisted strategy was concocted. So stop pulling my chain. Numbers and locations, or I feed you to the monsters floating in Lake Erie. The ones you brought to my city."

That threat raised Williams' willingness to talk tenfold. Albright had shown that BSU prisoners would find no quarter in RAM. The rules had changed; his life was only worth the knowledge he had. And if he shared that knowledge it would be worth nothing.

Realization smacked the haze from his mind. What life was he protecting? He'd fed a man to the dead, for God's sake. His warring mind promised to split his skull. His past life raged as it lost its grip on today's reality.

"Get me a pen and paper. I'd like to leave my blighted existence saving someone for a change. The first thing you want to do is close the wall breach between Nevada and Utah."

Albright pulled Williams to his feet and slammed him into a blood-soaked interrogation chair. He slapped a notepad and pen in front of the battered man. "Total force size. Targets outside of Cleveland. Tactics used to infiltrate those targets. All the BSU leaders involved. Start writing and you'll live."

Williams craned his neck in Albright's direction. Only fuzzy edges of his interrogator were visible through swollen eyes. He towered over Williams, backlit by a single light bulb dangling from the ceiling, and ready to strike. "I'm not sure I deserve to live."

Chapter 47
Crossover

Willis, Lewis, and Stevenson arrived exactly two hours after talking to Otto. Dillan dragged himself from the rickety lawn chair positioned directly in front of the main gate and granted them access.

The clatter arising from the men building the secondary gate drowned out Willis' greeting to an exhausted Dillan.

The double gate system was the starting point for improving their fence security. It would allow visitors access to a holding pen for safety, while limiting the risk of combatants escaping into the community to wreak havoc. Visitors would enter a forty by forty-foot fenced area. The first gate would then be closed, allowing security to inspect and disarm them. If they passed, the second gate would be opened, granting access to the community.

"Hey, Willis. We've been waiting for you. If you'd been late, I was going to abandon my post and get some sleep. I told the crew that no one gets in unless I let them in, so you'd have been waiting for a long while."

Regarding the dark bags under Dillan's eyes, Willis asked, "When was the last time you slept, Dillan?"

"It feels like the last Tuesday of May 2005. But I think it was actually two days ago. After you defuse the wired-up UCs, I'm going to try to catch forty winks."

Willis observed the flurry of activity inside the community. A community that once felt safe from the horrors outside its fence now resembled a Forward Operating Base in Kandahar, Afghanistan. Men, women, and children labored at assigned tasks, orders were given, and urgency bled from their bodies. But something stood out above all else: Unity! If one faltered, another took up the slack; if one fell, another pulled them to their feet. These people weren't going to quit.

This bastion of survivors had no intention of surrendering an inch of this community. Instead, they leaned into the challenge and pushed back with a collective force that awed Willis. He needed this in his life; he needed to surround himself with fighters.

And the seed was sown.

"Who lit the fire?" Willis asked.

"The fire has always burned; Otto just stoked it into an inferno. He showed every single one of us what it will take to live."

Willis looked a question at Dillan. "Yes, Otto. Otto Hammer flipped the apocalypse off. Then the crazy bastard asked this entire community to join him, and they did."

"Are we talking about the same Otto?" Willis asked. "The same Otto who was stuck in a chair earlier today? Who I refused to issue hand grenades so he didn't accidentally kill us all? The Otto who claimed medical supplies and solar panels were a waste of time? That Otto?"

Dillan managed a weak smile and said, "That's the one. Now, if he could just remember people's names, he might get Pat to stop yelling at him."

It shocked Willis, no, dumbfounded him. He liked Otto, and his spirit was unquestionable, but Otto Hammer being *inspirational?* Not a chance. Nevertheless, his eyes weren't lying, these people were motivated. Moreover, they seemed to be taking pleasure performing the back-breaking work. *I've seen it all!*

"So, where is his royal self? I need to talk to him about your prisoner."

Dillan's smile faded at the mention of the BSU prisoner. "You'll find that little puke on the southeast corner. Lisa and Otto are talking to him."

Willis caught the phrasing but thought Dillan misspoke. He thanked Dillan and climbed back into the Hummer. "Stevenson, let's find Otto!"

"Lisa, I'm sorry to interrupt. But I hear the harmonic tones of a Hummer approaching."

Her body glistening in the early evening sun, Lisa stopped mid-swing at the news of the Hummer. Then, thinking better of it, mustered the last of her energy and let her right-cross fly. Her follow-through carried her slightly off balance as the man strung to the fence lost consciousness when her fist, wrapped tightly in leather, shattered his left eye socket.

Exhausted and sticky from her enemy's blood, she gazed at the man hanging from the fence from his bound arms. "Otto, did you write down all the information he gave us? Or should I wake him and ask for more?"

"I think we have enough, Lisa. And Willis asked me to ensure he was still breathing when they picked him up."

I was numb to the tactics Lisa had employed. She took over about five minutes into the *conversation*. I started the interrogation thinking we'd work the good cop bad cop routine on him. But he decided to negotiate with us. He seemed to have forgotten the fate his friend suffered when he withheld information. Maybe he figured the circumstances were different or that because he helped us identify the terrorist zombie, we'd go easy on him. Whatever his motivation, it was a terrible strategy.

Lisa landed her first punch after he said he'd tell us if we gave him food and water. The vicious blow split his upper lip wide open. The man's crying seemed to enrage Lisa, and she launched a barrage of kicks and punches, moving so fast her body became a blur. As I watched, the Tasmanian Devil of Saturday morning cartoon fame came to mind.

My instinct was to stop her, to slow it down. But I realized I didn't care about him. Hell, I didn't even care if we got any information at all. We'd been the nail long enough; today we became the hammer. So I took a seat on a woodpile, pulled out my notepad, and let Lisa work.

The anger she unleashed was fascinating to witness. The more he wept, the harder she hit him. He spewed the information she asked for, but it didn't matter, she still beat him. Lisa would stop only long enough for him to finish a sentence before reopening her can of whoop-ass on him.

After about thirty minutes, he figured out that the longer he talked, the longer he spared himself from Lisa's rage. It didn't work out well for him when she realized what he was doing.

Four things happened at once: his mouth filled with too much blood for him to speak, Lisa lined up her last punch, the Hummer approached our position, and I realized how much anger Lisa holds. I'm thankful she plays for my team.

"Otto, he's breathing right?" Willis asked while he approached our position.

"You'll want to check his pulse, but he was breathing three minutes ago. He's also going to require a lot of stitches. The dumbass kept falling down and smacking his face, neck, abdomen, and groin on the ground. Then we helped him out and strung him to the fence. But, you'll notice, we were too late to keep him from hurting himself."

Ignoring my explanation, Willis pointed to the notepad and asked, "Is that scribble the INTEL he gave you in exchange for you all taking such wonderful care of him?"

"All yours, Willis," I said as I handed it to him. "I've committed most of it to memory. You'll want to act on it before we do."

Willis nodded and took my notepad, glanced at Stevenson, and said, "Cut the prisoner loose. He'll be executed at Hopkins with the other prisoners."

The BSU soldier was on the ground before my brain registered Willis' words.

Willis addressed our shock. "New orders. RAM isn't taking any more prisoners."

Lisa approached the motionless husk and leaned over for an inspection of the damage wreaked by her handiwork. Her reaction indicated we had crossed a line in our fight. She shrugged her shoulders and muttered, "Meh."

Combatants be advised, your life means nothing.

"Willis, has RAM stopped taking refugees and combatants or only combatants?" I asked.

"Otto, orders are to extract as much information as possible from non-RAM persons. Determine their intent. Send non-hostiles to our interior holding camps. Honestly, Otto, I don't think it's a sustainable strategy. The entry points are shutting down because the buildups have become unmanageable. The UCs are drawn to the gates and devour survivors while they wait to enter RAM. Entry Point One has been locked down. The breach at Entry Point Four is sealed, but they were also forced to cut off access from BSU. Both have commenced with bombardment. We've been able to airlift small numbers of survivors to safety, but yesterday one turned during the return flight. That incident cost RAM four Airmen, a pilot, copilot, and twelve civilians, not to mention the Black Hawk. That'll mark the end to airlifts. So, the short of it is: Resources are dictating we no longer perform search and rescue outside RAM borders."

Willis, jaw set tight, glanced at Stevenson and Lewis and said, "Otto, the Entry Points that are still operating are reporting less than ten people a day surviving the massacres at their gates. BSU is lost, Otto. Our drones find fewer and fewer pockets of survivors every day. The war is lost in BSU. We need to focus only on saving RAM."

I think I was more disturbed by my reaction. Although troubled by the revelation, and saddened at the loss of human life, I was more worried about our resources.

I started to speak but Willis cut in, "Where are the suicide UCs located? We don't have a demolition specialist with us. We're planning to detonate them."

We had just fought to stop them from blowing up our community, so purposely blowing them up was a backwards idea. "Willis, not a chance you're detonating them this close to my home. That plan sucks. Come at me with a better option."

Willis managed a smile and said, "Relax, Otto, we've done this before. We brought sandbags to cover them and direct the blast away from the fence and your home. Just get everyone behind cover. We need to wrap this up, then rally with the VP's security detail for tonight's visit."

I got on the radio and contacted Pat, Al, and Darline. I told them of the plan and asked they get everyone to take cover. I gave them fifteen minutes to do it. I had to shut off my radio when Pat expressed her displeasure with the compressed timeline. Even with everything that just happened, Pat was still intimidating as ever!

Lewis gave a soft chuckle at my reaction, then said, "Speaking of Pat. The hospital wants a POC for updates on your wounded and Andy's blood test results. I was going to designate Pat, but I'm not sure how that'll play for the person from the hospital. How about Durrell and Sabrina?"

"Give all three of them as the POCs," Lisa chirped. "Pat has a strong desire to be plugged into the goings-on of the community. And I sure wouldn't want to be the one blamed for leaving her out of the loop."

Lisa spoke the truth; I would never live it down if I cut her out of the information stream. Lewis raised his eyebrows, as if remembering a traumatic experience, and nodded his approval. We gave him the channel that Durrell, Sabrina, and Pat monitored and left it at that.

Lisa accompanied me on my walk home. We were quiet until the halfway point when I asked, "Hey, Sis. Did we cross a line? The one I've read about in all my zombie books that marks the crossover to our devolution into uncaring, hardhearted subhumans that attack old people for their food stashes?"

Cutting a hard look at me, Lisa said, "You go soft on me now, Hammer, and I'll kick your ass in front of this entire community. What we did today, as ugly as it was, had to happen. And it won't be the last time we'll be forced to do horrendous things. But our actions will keep us alive. And if you start crying when things get tough, I'll be sure to give you something to cry about."

"Lisa, thanks for the *pep* talk. I almost forgot. I wanted to talk to you about the MST directive. We need to…"

Two massive explosions rattled our home as Willis and his men detonated the UC terrorists.

Chapter 48
VIPVP

Willis, Lewis, and Stevenson arrived at the main gate forty minutes ahead of VP Pace's security detail. They remained outside the gate with Stevenson manning the Hummer's turret gun. Their posture was forceful and bristled with the anticipation of violence.

With newly issued suppressed M4s, Willis and Lewis cleared a few UCs that loitered in the area after the disturbance from earlier and the team's arrival.

I observed their methodical and efficient work from behind the gate and realized that even though they utilized suppressed weapons, the M4s still produced an easily heard report. The intent, I surmised, was to avoid drawing monsters from further away to our location and to cut down on the battering their ears were taking during this war.

I also realized I wanted to add a suppressor to my AR, actually to all of our weapons. When the threats were eliminated, I called out, "Willis, how do I go about securing ten or twenty of those suppressors?"

Willis answered while approaching the fence, "Well, you need to buy a tax stamp, fill out the Form 4, and send it to the ATF. Then, wait for about... forever. Then you get to pick it up."

"Not cool, Willis, not cool at all."

Unable to contain his smile, Willis responded, "Otto, no one has ever accused me of being a cool guy." His face went stony and he said, "I'd like to talk to you about something. You got a second?"

"Not for un-cool guys, so write me a note and wait for my reply. I'll try to be quick about it."

I pulled away from the gate and turned for home when Willis asked again, with a little more urgency, "Otto, I need to ask you a question. So, hold up. I'm coming in."

I pulled to a stop and waited for him to catch up to me. In a hushed tone, the question he asked caught me off guard. "How many homes are empty in your community?"

My eyes narrowed. "Who wants to know?"

"Me, Lewis, and Stevenson want to know. Look, Otto, we have family in the Canton safe zone, and we want to move them to your community. And, before you ask, you'll understand why after the VP is done with his speech. So, would your community accept our families?"

"Willis, everyone is welcome, and your families aren't an exception to that rule. We have more than enough housing. Make certain they understand we assign every community member a job. And in addition, we all contribute time to our security. If they're okay with that, they can live here."

"What's your job, Otto? Phys-Ed Instructor or Professional Complainer?"

"Ha. Ha. Ha. You're so funny, Willis. I forgot to laugh," I shot back.

Willis stuffed a laugh and said, "But, you did just kind of laugh—."

I cut in because he was right, and I wasn't happy about it. "WILLIS, bring your family before I change my mind. I'll tell Pat. Anything else?"

Willis, again stone-faced, said, "My enlistment ends in thirty days. I could be an asset."

My shock and question were cut off by the crackle from Willis' radio, "VIPVP security detail for advanced force Willis Whip, how copy?"

"Willis Whip, who came up with that call sign?" I sniggered.

Red-faced, Willis grabbed his radio, met my amused stare, and told me, "No time to talk, I'll see you at the speech in an hour."

CHAPTER 49
BLACKMAIL?

The summer sun was disappearing behind a row of evergreens when the enormous tour bus rolled through our main gate. Dillan, refreshed after a few hours of shuteye, wasn't thrilled that he couldn't perform a bite check on the inhabitants. The guarantee that no one would exit the bus seemed to appease him, and he granted them entry.

The bus filled the intersection at the end of my street as its idling engine stood ready to whisk its precious cargo away at a moment's notice.

I visually inspected the impressive vehicle as the residents took up positions on the broadside of the bus that faced east, as we were directed to do by the VP's security detail. Darline, Lisa, Randy, and Nila, followed by my brothers and their wives, joined me near the front of the crowd.

Access to the bus was restricted and a fifteen-foot perimeter was established around the entirety of the behemoth. Willis and his men flanked it to our right while two hard-looking men flanked it to our left.

Stone registered the security and our vulnerable position the same time Randy did. "I don't like it," Stone said. "It would only take about twenty-five seconds to kill every one of us." Randy nodded his agreement with Stone's assessment.

"Already on it," I said. "You'll notice Dillan and half of his security detail are missing. I issued them the M249 and M4s and put them in over-watch positions. If it goes sideways, we have a fighting chance."

I was greeted with stunned silence. "What? I'm too stupid to devise a solid strategy? I'm not hooked up to life-support with a barely functioning brain for God's sake." Nothing changed; just blank stares and stunned silence. "I hope you both get bitten, ya pricks."

That got their attention. It also elicited some depraved retorts, like *"We should have left you in Terra Alta,"* and, *"Old and mean don't look good on you,"* and *"Your brain really is broken,"* but my favorite was, *"Next time we'll tell Lisa to leave you for the UCs!"* I couldn't tell who said what because the insults were launched at me like a hive of angry bees defending their honey!

As I developed my decidedly abrasive response to the despicable insults hurled at me, I detected movement from the corner of my eye. The crowd fell silent as the slight movement morphed into the side of the bus *unfolding*. "Holy shit, a Transformer ate the VP," I whispered, prompting Darline to poke me in the ribs again.

The hiss of hydraulic pistons and swoosh of weather-tight seals separating filled the humid summer air and transfixed the crowd. Randy leaned into Stone (probably because he wasn't talking to me again) and said, "If it's going to happen, it'll happen now."

The three of us simultaneously placed our hands on our sidearms. As the side panels locked into place, an enormous monitor was revealed. "I need one of those. Think Willis can get one for us?" I asked Randy, who made a show of ignoring my question. *This guy!*

An instant later, light and sound burst from the monitor as a familiar face materialized on the screen. Static and squelch battled for control over the sound system as the crowd grew restless with the delay.

The picture and sound blinked twice and stabilized on VP Pace's face. His easy smile and confident stature were exactly what we needed from our leaders. But then, he delivered his message, "Good evening to all of you. Thank you for allowing us to join you this evening. I will not insult your intelligence with empty words, citing progress that doesn't exist. Our war against the UC hordes is relentless and being fought on multiple fronts."

As he gathered his thoughts, someone in the crowd yelled, "Thanks for the update, Captain Obvious."

Under normal circumstances, I would berate the owner of those words. But today, I agreed fully with their heckling comment. Although not fighting on the front lines for RAM, we sure as hell were on the front lines in our world. We too fought multiple battles on multiple fronts and lost friends and loved ones. We pushed ourselves to the breaking point every day. So, yep we knew it was bad… Captain Obvious!

Only slightly fazed by the outburst, Pace continued. "Well, I guess I had that coming and I apologize for my thoughtless comment. We're all fighting this battle; we've all lost at some level. If not for you, the citizens of this magnificent country, we would have been overrun weeks ago. Thank you for fighting!"

What he said pumped a few chests with air.

He continued, "I have information for all of you. I know we've been slow to update our national broadcasts and occasionally we've lost our ability to broadcast via television. We're working around the clock to keep those recourses active and current, but our teams are overwhelmed and unable to meet all the demands."

After a quick look off-screen followed by a rapid and hushed conference with an unseen adviser, Pace again focused his attention on us. "Let me get started so you fine people can get back to the lives you've carved out for yourselves. RAM has cleared and secured all of our nuclear power plants. We are short on qualified technicians to operate them at full capacity, but several are currently online." I breathed out for a long time after he told us about the nuclear plants. And Stone placed a firm grip on my shoulder when he noticed my reaction.

"The coal-fired and natural gas power plants will be offline shortly due to supply chain interruptions. Meaning, our ability to supply power will be limited and will cause sporadic and rolling brownouts until we ramp the nuclear plants up to full capacity. If any portion of the power grid is compromised, our response will be severely delayed."

At this point I whipped out my notepad and pen and began scribbling notes and questions. Darline whispered, "What are you doing? Are they going to allow a Q&A?"

"I don't think he knows it yet. But I'm going to ask questions, Darline. When have you ever known me not to ask questions?"

"Otto, please don't. The way you ask questions makes people uncomfortable. It's like you're a shark and the person you're asking is chum in the water."

She's not wrong; I can be a little aggressive when I ask questions. But if you prefer not to answer questions, stop speaking. It really is that simple.

"Sorry, chick, this is too important. And I'll remind you, he's the VP of RAM. He should be ready to answer questions at any second, regarding anything."

Jack shushed us and pointed to his eyes, then to the screen. Informing us he was *very* interested in Pace's speech, so please be quiet. He's done the same thing since we were kids!

Darline went to her tip-toes and whispered, "Please, please, pretty please don't do it."

But I remained focused on my notes and the VP.

"You've probably noticed the behavioral changes in the UCs, including that terrible rasping noise and the semblance of motor skills. We're studying these developments and have news to share. The rasping seems to be a mechanism for flushing out their quarry. Our reports indicate that they make it, most often, when they lose sight of humans or attempt to force humans to change direction and move into a better tactical position for hunting. If you are hiding from them, and you hear that noise, remain still. Much like a wolf pack, they force you toward their silent hunting partners, striking once you're in position. Remember this information; it may save your life."

I looked at Darline and waggled my notepad and, in my best singsong whisper voice, said, "Neener, neener, neener, I'm not sharing my notes with you!" My ribs, apparently her new favorite target, were so black and blue I looked like a mule had kicked me. And the attack my song elicited from her dainty little fingers, forged from carbon steel, caused me searing pain and a sharp yelp!

My reaction garnered the attention of the security detail, caused the VP to stop mid-sentence, and earned sharp looks from the crowd. With the white-hot spotlight of embarrassment shining brightly on my thinning hairline, I felt like a burning matchstick. Hands raised in mock surrender, I said, "It's Darline's fault. Sorry, please proceed." That earned me another shot from Darline's deadly little digits!

I decided that my wife was being unnecessarily abusive, so I moved away from her and closer to the aisle that had formed as the crowd filtered in. This would prove to be a fatal flaw on behalf of my lovely wife.

The VP held for a second before continuing. "I'm going to go through the rest of my talking points in bullet point fashion; we have many stops to make and want to visit everyone as quickly as possible. President Train is secured in an undisclosed location while fully engaged in serving our country. St. Joe's Hospital has been converted into a military base. We located dozens of communities, like yours, throughout RAM. Just prior to our visit, we confirmed strongholds in Parma and Akron. We will supply you a list of other survivors and their locations. We identified the source of the heinous attacks carried out by BSU operatives and have commenced countermeasures. I'm so very sorry for the losses they've caused your community. To ensure the safety of the civilian inhabitance, we are relocating all safe zones to RAM's interior states. You are still welcome to migrate to them; be advised, if you do you will no longer live in Ohio."

The crowd bristled at the news of the safe zones being relocated. I believe many of them received it as a removal of a fallback option. A place to live if our fences failed. Now, the safety zones were gone, and hard choices needed to be made. Did they remain in their homes or move to a new state, cut off from their friends and family with no easy way back home. Anxiety coursed through the residents like a jolt of electricity and I began to worry about the long-term viability of our home. If our population dwindled further, it would spell the community's end. Well, the end for some. I didn't plan on leaving!

What he said next sucked the air out of the crowd. "Humanity is on the brink of extinction. We hold a vicarious grip on our slice of the world. We are unable to give you an exact death toll, but estimates place it at seventy-five percent worldwide. We will be ramping up the use of the MST program. We will ask them to go further from home, support the troops at the Entry Points, and at times launch assaults on our enemies."

My hand went up faster than Horshack with an answer. Darline face-palmed while Stone, Randy, and Jack appeared to pray. "Excuse me, Mister Vice President, I have a question. As an MST member, I need to know who decided to change direction. Better yet, why the hell didn't anyone consult the members of said MST? We've already lost a friend due to the poor planning and execution of this *relationship*."

My chest heaved with a growing anger. "What if we decide that we don't care for your plan? What happens then?"

I paused for a breath and Pace cut in, "You're Otto Hammer, aren't you?"

Rattled that he referred to me by name, I replied with a moderately civil, "Yes. I'm Otto. Who told you my name?"

"Oh, I was briefed on you. Your reputation precedes you." A smile pulled the corners of his mouth.

I shot a look at a shocked Willis; he appeared as surprised as me. "Yeah, well, it's my effervescent personality. Please answer my question. What happens if we refuse?"

"Mister Hammer, we can't guarantee your safety or supply your community without the MST's support."

My head nearly exploded! He was blackmailing us!

A sharp turn to my right found Darline, Jackson, Stone, and Randy looking at me with pleading eyes. They understood what was happening in my head and that it wouldn't end well! My long-held belief was that blackmailers should be killed. My logic was this: Blackmail never stops. If you have done something so damning that you'll pay to keep it a secret then you'll pay forever. It only ends when the life of the blackmailer ends.

"Is he blackmailing us?" I asked my tense-faced friends and family.

Not waiting for a response, I launched my verbal attack. Free of Darline's deadly digits, I was also able to approach the bus unfettered. "I'm sorry, are you *blackmailing* us? Did you just tell..."

Randy interrupted my tirade, "Otto, it's not blackmail."

Darline chimed in, "It's extortion, Otto. I've explained the difference a hundred times!"

Jack tossed in his couple of cents, "Otto, the nice men with guns aren't happy with you."

Stone decided to fuel the fire, "Its blackmail, Otto. Or maybe extortion? Probably both. Go with both!"

Darline's eyes drilled holes into Stone's head and she asked, "Why, Stone? Why did you do that?"

Stone shrugged. "Very hard to tell. But it seemed like fun. Bad timing?"

I turned my attention back to the bus. "Hey, you know what? We don't need you or your *support* or *guarantees*! We've done fine without government intervention. And another thing, except for the food, medical supplies, guns, and Hummer, you can have it all back..."

"It's a Humvee, Otto," Pace interjected while I gulped air.

With balled fists and flared nostrils, I moved towards the bus. This time my brothers intervened, each grabbing an arm and pulling me away from the gathering. Oh, I wasn't done; they'd just stopped me from getting killed!

"Hummer, Humvee, Humdinger, I don't care. We're keeping it and our independence. I hereby declare this community an independent state. A state defended by FST1, Freedom Support Team One and the sovereign people of this community."

Darline and Randy fell in step as I was hauled away from the meeting. Pat stepped up and asked the VP to continue his speech. But I noticed she didn't apologize; her face told me something. She was proud!

"I see the reports on Otto were accurate. He's a…"

Pat sliced through his comment, "Mister Pace, Otto is a leader of this community. That's all you need to know. So, please continue with your prepared remarks. This independent state has work to do."

Chapter 50
This Changes Everything

Pat entered her home, exhaustion battling her exhilaration for control. "Otto, you crazy son of a bit—." Her declaration was interrupted by a voice coming from her radio.

"This is Doctor McCune from Saint Joe's calling Patric... err, Pat Schreiber or Sabrina and Durrell Adams. Please respond." The voice was filled with a confident poise that Pat found unsettling.

Pat snatched the radio from her belt and responded, "Pat here. Do you have an update?"

"Nice to speak with you, Pat. I do have an update. One of your wounded, Andros, will return home by week's end. Bill, however, will remain hospitalized. His injuries are significant and we're struggling to stabilize him."

Sabrina broke in after the doctor finished, "Sabrina here. I heard the update; what's Bills prognosis?"

"Sabrina, I'm pleased to have the opportunity to speak with you. You and your husband are the attending physicians, correct?"

"That's an overstatement, Doctor. We are medics and tried our best with limited resources."

The doctor said, "You took excellent care of your patients. You should be proud of the work you performed. Unfortunately, his prognosis is grim. We've done all we can. It's now his fight to win."

The news silenced Pat and Sabrina. They couldn't lose another member of the community.

"Doctor, fix him," Pat commanded before her emotions overtook her.

After a lengthy silence, the doctor continued without addressing Pat's directive, "I have excellent news regarding the blood sample. Confusing, but good news. We identified that several conditions contributed to the donor's virus test kit results and perplexing symptoms. I'll give you a moment to secure a pen and paper."

Pat immediately responded, "Go."

"The donor has a form of Hyperthyroidism never seen before today. It's causing his increased energy and physical wellness and may be the contributing factor to his subnormal body temperature. His skin tone is caused, as best we can determine, by a severe case of Tinea Versicolor. Other than that, his blood work indicates he's healthier than any human ever tested. Quite remarkable, actually."

Sabrina quickly asked, "What are our treatment options?"

"Treat the Versicolor with any antifungal shampoo, like a Selsun Blue, Nizoral, or Head and Shoulders. That should clear it up in short order. The thyroid is different; we may need to admit him into the hospital for further treatment and observation. We want to administer a combination of drugs, methimazole, and propranolol to be exact."

Pat didn't like it; the doctor was too quick to offer a bed to someone with minor ailments during the apocalypse. She was sure the community had those medications from the drugstore they had scavenged. "We're okay, Doctor, we can treat him here. Anything else?"

The extremely long silence told Pat her suspicion was correct. The good doctor wanted more.

"Well, um, your recovered person will be home by week's end; we'll arrange military transport. Can you pull another vial of blood from Mr., I'm sorry, I don't know his name."

"We can supply another vial when you deliver the others to us. Thank you for your time. Sabrina and I are signing off." With that, she shut off her radio.

Doctor McCune placed the silent radio on the lab table next to the microscope. He took another look at the sample on the slide, adjusting the microscope to one-hundred-time magnification. It was happening. The activity was undeniable.

He reached for his sat-phone and dialed it, knowing this call would change everything.

The phone rang once. When the line picked up he didn't wait for salutations from the man on the other end. "I have very important news regarding the sample."

**To be continued in *A Dangerous Freedom*
Coming in Fall/Winter 2020**

Thanks for reading! I'd like to thank all of my friends and family for their support. And a special thanks to Heidi, Darline, and you, the reader! Without you, none of this is possible.

Reviews are valuable to independent writers. Please consider leaving yours where you purchased this book. Please feel free to like Otto Hammer Book, on Facebook, where the story continues.

You'll only lose on the days you don't remind yourself that you are, in fact, the STORM!

Book One in the Divided America Zombie Apocalypse series is available on Amazon.

AUTHOR'S BIOGRAPHY

Hello! I'm supposed to tell you a little about myself, so here we go. I bet you can't wait! I was born in Cleveland, Ohio. I now live in NEO (North East Ohio) with my wonderful wife (she told me to say that). Our beautiful daughter lives in California with her extraordinary husband, and we miss them every day.

In my early adult life I spent time as a Repo-Man for a rent-to-own furniture company, a bill collector, and a heavy drinker. Then I pulled myself together and spent twenty-seven years working my way through sales management in corporate America. However, one day, I was sitting in a meeting and the right person said the right thing at the right time and I realized enough was truly enough. I've always wanted to do this, write a book, and I realized that we, you and me, have about fifteen minutes on the face of this planet and I needed to do one of the things I had always wanted to do. And, well, this is it.

If you're wondering, yes, I'm a conservative, I own guns, and I hate paying taxes.

My hope is that one day you're sitting in a meeting, delivering a package, serving someone dinner, or doing whatever it is you do for a living and decide that enough is enough. It's the scariest thing you'll ever do. But I promise at no point in your life will you feel more alive than the day you take control of the life you're living!

Made in the USA
Middletown, DE
10 July 2020